Ashes and the Legend of Stormracer

Vaughn Hansen

Over the Dunes Press - Lamar, IN
ISBN: 979-8-3304-1031-6
Ashes and the Legend of Stormracer
Vaughn Hansen.
Available formats: eBook | Paperback distribution

Second Edition 2024

Dedication

I this book is dedicated to my sister Amy Hansen and my publisher without whose help it would not have been possible. Also to Claire Franzman and Shelly Goodrich who designed the cover art. And with great love to the Animals who we share are lives with now or who are waiting for us in the next life.

Authors note

All the people, places and landmarks mentioned in this book are named in honor of the Animals in our lives both now and those who have crossed the rainbow bridge.

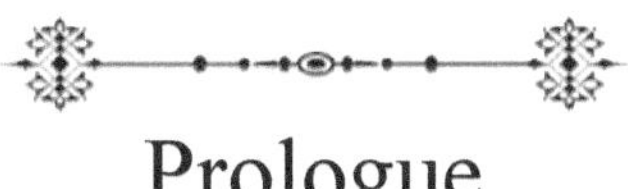

Prologue

Domino's footsteps echoed as he walked through the empty halls of the huge castle. It was hard for him to believe that just weeks ago these same hallways had been busy with servants and townspeople going about their business. Now except for himself and Shilo, the once great lands-queen, there was only one other person remaining in the castle.

Despite the growing heat outside, the hallways were cold and dark as if the castle itself knew of the curse that had taken over the kingdom. Like the land around it the entire castle had changed becoming a place of despair and emptiness that he no longer recognized.

Walking by his side Shilo moved closer to him sensing her uneasiness he put a comforting hand on her shoulder. Glancing over at him Shilo muttered, "You know nothing we say is going to make a difference he won't change his mind he is not going to go with us."

"I know", Domino answered, "but we have to try he is my brother and your husband. We can't just leave him here no matter what he has done. We have to try to talk some sense into him. Make him see that Molder played on his pain and anger of our mother's death and used him for his own means this was not his doing alone."

A deep sorrow showed in Shilo's eyes as she stopped to look out one of the many hallway windows facing the courtyard. The courtyard itself stood unchanged the trees and garden seemingly untouched by the desert sun glaring down on it. A far different landscape stood on the other side of the castle wall.

Where once a river flowed from the green mountains into the rich fields and orchards of the valley, now only great sand covered dunes could be seen. Here and there a treetop with dry branches poked through the sand the only reminder of what once had been.

Domino looked out the window with her his hand still resting on her shoulder. "He still believes he can undo this, nothing we tried has made any difference the strongest sorcerers and the wisest mages have been helpless against the curse. I am not sure anything else can be done but he will not accept that."

Domino struck the wall next to the window startling Shilo, "His dam stubbornness and pride are to blame for all this! You would think that he would have learned from that, in some ways I fear my brother will never change!"

A new voice echoed down the hallway toward them. "Do you really think that brother? Do you really think that I have learned nothing from my stupidity? Our home and kingdom are no more our people have left cursing my name, beyond our borders people will not even speak this land's name out loud for fear of bringing down on their self the curse I have unleashed here. Do you really think so little of me to believe that I cannot see what I have done?"

Without waiting for an answer the man who had spoken turned and walked back into the room at the end of the hallway. Sighing, Domino followed with Shilo keeping pace beside him. The room at the end of the hallway was by far the largest in the castle, serving both as a dining hall and throne room. It could, and in days past, it had held over a thousand people. It's only occupant now stood in the middle of the great room staring at the painting covering the far wall. A painting of a horse of great beauty running across the cloud covered sky above the castle.

Standing with his back to them, the newcomer spoke again his voice ringing strangely hollow in the huge room. "You're leaving like the others I suppose?"

Shilo crossed the room putting her hand on his shoulder turning him to face her for a second a brief look of shock crossed her face as she looked up into the face of her husband hardly recognizing him.

He stood over a head taller than her with sandy brown hair, his face once always clean-shaven now covered with stubble, his filthy and ragged clothes showed he had not bothered to care for himself in many days.

And his once green eyes now seemed to shine with an inner light of their own making her take an involuntary step backward. "Have I really fallen so far in your eyes that you cannot stand to be near me, wife?"

Regaining her composer Shilo answered, "I will always stand by your Buck I love you nothing will ever change that."

A deep sadness showed in Buck's eyes as he put the back of his hand against the side of Shilo's face. "I love you to Shilo I never told you that as much as I should have and I am sorry about that. But you cannot stay here with me and I cannot go with you I have to undo what I have done. I have to bring her back somehow no matter how long it takes. I will return this land to what it once was, I must!"

Shilo answered him, "We are leaving and you are going with us, there is nothing left here Buck. There is nothing more that can be done, please! Come with us, we will start a new life somewhere else far from here where no one will ever know what happened. I forgive you Buck, Domino forgives you, Please come with us."

Buck looked over Shilo's head to his brother, "I am trusting you, little brother you are the only man I trust enough to keep her safe. Take whatever is left in the city treasury and whatever else you want. I will not be needing such things anymore."

Domino nodded his head. "When we find a new home I will send word somehow to let you know we are safe, and as long as I am able I will journey here the first month of summer every year to make sure there is nothing you need."

Looking back to Shilo's face Buck gave her a gentle kiss, "There is nothing I will need brother that the garden cannot give me and as long as I live, it will live. And as long as I do not stray far from these walls nothing, not even time can affect me. All I ask from you brother is that you love her like I do and take care of her."

Buck watched from the window of the great hallway as Domino and Shilo drove the heavy wagon down the sand covered road keeping his eyes on the wagon till it was swallowed up in the distance. "Goodbye Shilo, goodbye brother may God keep you safe." Turning back to the painting on the wall, he stared intently at it. "I will find a way to undo this somehow I promise

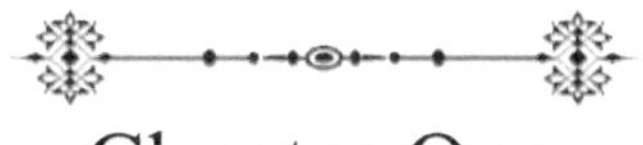

Chapter One
Fifteen Hundred Years Later

The sandstorm struck without warning.

A wall of wind and fury that nearly blew Ashes off his mount. Ducking his head against the wind, Ashes slid off his horse and unbuckled the saddlebags that were tied behind the saddle, squinting his eyes against the wind he dug threw them before finally pulling out his extra shirt. Shielding his eyes against the wind he moved to China's head and wrapped the shirt around the stallions head tucking the ends under the bridle to secure them from the wind.

The stallion stood for this indignity trusting his rider but not without an irritated snort. The shirt would protect his sensitive ears, eyes and muzzle from the windblown sand, but with his eyes covered he could not see and had to blindly follow Ashes lead. Having been together eight years and through many battles and hardships together the stallion trusted his rider completely.

Ashes could only duck his own head and try to shield his eyes with his free hand as he turned the stallion's rump to the wind and tried to get his bearings. Before the storm had struck they had been heading east toward the distant mountains still two days ride off.

Where with any luck he would find Summer, the women he had left many years ago believing that being a mercenary that he had nothing to offer her. Much had happened since then including him stumbling on a hidden oasis and finding a gem of great power granting him one wish.

In all honesty he still was not sure if what followed was real or a dream, but the effect it had on him was very real.

Having sworn off his life as a mercenary Ashes was determined to find Summer and regain the life he had so foolishly rode away from over twenty years ago. "Follow the sun three days from where you awaken and at the base of the tallest peak you will find her." The gem had told him that a day ago, now swallowed up by the storm the chances of reaching the mountains and Summer were growing smaller by the minute they had to find shelter soon.

Ashes struggled to see through the windblown sand, just before the storm had struck he had spotted a rocky ridge sticking up through the desert floor. If they could find it, it would provide them with the windbreak that they needed to survive the storm. There was no way of knowing for sure how far away the ridge was or in what direction, but it offered their only chance. Praying that his instincts were taking them in the right direction Ashes headed into the storm with China in tow.

He was just starting to think that they had been going in the wrong direction when they found the ridge. It was larger than it had looked at first stretching for over a mile in both directions and reaching over ninety feet high at its peak. Sensing that they were out of danger China tossed his head impatiently trying to free himself from the irritating thing clinging to his face, a stallion could only be asked to put up with so much.

He lowered his head for his rider to free him from his indignity rewarding the man with a messy snort to clear his nostrils of sand, if he was going to be inconvenienced so was his rider. It seemed only fair.

Glaring at the stallion Ashes used the shirt to clean his own face of the stallion's sign of discontent before putting the shirt back in the saddlebags. "You know I hear that a camel can travel the desert for days without needing any water and a sandstorm would hardly slow them down. If I were you I would start showing my rider more respect or I might remember that next time we are in the marketplace and decide to see if there is any truth to that rumor. I hear that horse meat is selling well in Tangra."

Unconcerned China dropped his head looking for any unsuspecting blades of grass that dared to poke their heads above the sand. Ashes pulled off the saddle and bridle letting the stallion wander under the shelter of the ridge before making camp.

Having crossed this desert twice before in the past, he knew very well how big these storms could get. They could easily end up spending the night or longer under the ridge. Annoyed at the delay in reuniting with Summer he started rummaging through the large bag of fruit from the oasis finally pulling out several large setas, a hard to find strange looking pear-shaped fruit with a leathery skin which served to protect the fruit from insects and other harm. The skin made it hard to peel even with a sharp knife though most people agreed that the prize was worth the effort. The inner meat was so sweet that a single fruit could bring as much as a good horse in the marketplace.

Ashes used his knife to strip off the fruits tough skin, tossing the peelings in China's direction. The stallion's strong teeth and jaws having little trouble with them. The ridge blocked some of the wind and sand but not all and Ashes knew that this was a temporary shelter at best. For now it would have to do.

Finding a flat boulder to sit on he ate his fruit as he watched China shifting through the sand for the peelings when he felt a cold breeze on his cheek. Glancing over his shoulder, at first he did not see the crevice the wall behind him looked unbroken and solid. Then he felt the breeze again stronger this time making the hairs on the back of his neck rise up.

The feeling had nothing to do with the breeze, he could not rid himself of the feeling that something was watching them.

China seemed to share his feelings the stallion had stopped nosing through the sand and was staring hard at the cliff wall behind him, flattening his ears.

"Easy stud", Ashes muttered sliding his sword out of the sheath and slipping off the rock he had been sitting on he moved closer to the cliff wall eyeing it warily. At first he did not see the source of the breeze the wall looked unbroken the face of the ledge looked solid even from a few feet away. But a closer inspection revealed the truth, one side of the cliff face stood away from its brother overlapping it by several feet, leaving a hidden opening a horse width wide leading into a dark cave entrance. The cold breeze coming from the dark tunnel hinted that the cave on the other side was a good sized one. He had little love for caves. He preferred the open sky above his head and a clear view of his surroundings over the dark dampness of a cave.

It would be foolishness to ignore the dark opening. The chances that anyone or anything was lurking inside was small but he had known many a good man who had been killed by small chances. Cursing himself for his childlike fears he headed through the tunnel into the dark cave opening. China's worried nicker followed him as he stepped into the darkness then like a door closing the sounds of the storm were swallowed by the dark heavy silence.

Ashes shot a quick look over his shoulder to make sure that the entrance was still there before slowly making his way further into the cave. He had only gone a few feet when the floor suddenly made a sharp downward slope, feeling with his feet he worked his way down the trail. A hundred feet further the ground leveled out again but the darkness clung to him like a living thing.

Looking back the way he had come Ashes felt a moment of concern when he could not see the cave entrance, then he spotted the dim outline of the opening in the darkness. Retracing his steps he hurried back the way he had come not wanting to risk the storm blocking the light and trapping him inside the cave. He had heard stories of men who had lost their way in a cave never to find their way out again and he had no wish to join them.

Stepping back thru the cave entrance his relief was short lived, like passing into another world the sudden light and roar of the wind were almost overwhelming. The darkening sky was not an evening light as he had hoped it was much worse. Like a living thing the storm had grown and the wind shifted in the short time he had been in the cave, he could barely make out China's outline as the horse stood with his back to the storm facing him. Digging through the sand he grabbed his saddlebags and supplies dragging the saddle with one hand he called to China.

"Come on, horse. I'm not going to carry you. Move it, before you get buried!"

Snorting China followed only to stop at the narrow tunnel blowing loudly. His legs locked and the whites of his eyes showing as he eyed the dark cave.

Throwing the supplies into the cave Ashes squeezed past the horse and the rock wall using the flat of his sword he gave the stallion a hard swat on the back of his legs. 'Move it, stud! After all, we've been through I am not going to lose you to a damn storm, get going!"

Squealing in protest China leaped into the cave his sides brushing on both sides as he passed through the narrow tunnel. Once he was inside the cave China spun on his hooves to face the man coming through the entrance behind him that had dared to strike him in such a manner.

Unworried Ashes pushed past the horse. "Yeah, I know, you're mad but you will get over it. Would you rather be buried alive by the storm?" Picking up the saddlebags, Ashes dug his spare shirt out again before sitting it back on the cave floor. Reaching over his back he unsheathed one of his swords and wrapped the shirt tightly around the end of the blade, then fumbled around through the supply bag for a minute before he found the small bottle of oil he kept to keep the rust off his swords.

Such oil could be hard to find and he hated the thought of wasting it but the darkness of the cave gave him little choice. Turning the sword slowly he uncorked the bottle and poured half the oil on to the shirt before putting the cork back and sitting the bottle back into the bag. Then pulling out his flint and stone he offered a silent prayer of thanks when the oil caught after only a few strikes casting a flickering light on the cave floor. Holding the torch high above his head Ashes turned a slow circle.

The light from the torch flickered across the cave floor and the mouth of the cave they came through. But not far enough to reach the far walls, the breeze coming from the darkness beyond fanned the flames hinting that the cave was indeed far bigger than he had first thought. Sitting the torch against a rock he threw the saddle and supplies back on China's back and tightened the cinch and gathered up the reins before picking up the torch and starting down the path he had followed earlier.

If anything the light made the cave more forbidding as Ashes and China made their way down the steep incline. Ashes almost preferred the total darkness to the eerie shadows that danced in front of them.

China's soft blowing and his ridged steps showed that he shared Ashes sediments. As they neared the bottom, a rock clattered echoing in the darkness and China suddenly stopped pulling the reins hard as he jerked his head sideways to stare intently at a large boulder just beyond the torches light. In a single move Ashes dropped the reins and pulled his spare sword free from its scabbard he knew the stallion too well and trusted him even spooked the horse would not start for no reason.

Holding the torch higher he made his way around the dark bolder his sword ready, the ground around the huge rock was sandy and covered in strange furrows but nothing moved. Ashes was squatting down to inspect a large hole on the far side when something caught his boot almost tripping him.

Cursing he jerked his foot back and swung the torch around to see what had grabbed him. A large branch the size of a man's thigh stuck out of the sand, using his boot he pushed against it.

A loud snap filled the cave as the branch broke off just above the sand line, the wood was very old holding the torch above his head again he saw a similar sight in all directions. Some sticking higher than others but the entire cave floor was covered with wooden spikes sticking out of the ground.

Eyeing his tracks he could see that is was by pure chance he had passed thru the only clear path through the jungle of spikes. China's whinny echoed off the cave walls and Ashes could just make out the stallion's white form in the darkness. "Easy boy, I'm alright, but if you're saying you don't like this place then I am starting to agree with you the sooner we can get out of here the better."

The dark hole forgotten, Ashes retraced his steps back the way he came reaching China he gave the horse a soft pat on the neck and led him the last few feet down the incline then stripped off the saddle and supply bags.

"We will have to make camp till the storm passes so you might as well try to get some sleep I will keep watch I doubt I could sleep in this God forbidden place anyway." Looking around, he started gathering up some of the dry wood sticking above the cave floor "At least we will have a fire and some light, the torch is almost gone."

After stacking the wood in a pile shoved the torch into the dry wood watching as the flames lapped greedily at the dry fuel before pulling the sword back and shaking the burned shirt off into the fire. After shoving the glowing red end of the sword into the sand to cool it. He untied the end of the water bottle and carefully poured some water into his shield and watched as China drank for a minute before retiring the end of the bag.

Pulling the sword out of the sand and making sure it was cool Ashes dug out the bottle of oil again, after wiping the sand off the blade he uncorked the bottle and tilted it letting a small stream of oil run down the length of the blade twisting the blade over several times before using his fingers to spread the oil evenly. Re-corking the bottle he put it back in the supply bag working the oil into the blade for a few more minutes before returning it to its sheath.

China watched the man with one eye his ears kept moving listening for any strange sound. The stallion feared few things and nothing he could fight, but there was something about this place it had a darkness that went beyond sight that set the stallion's nerves on edge. There was something out there in the darkness beyond the fire that hooves and teeth could not touch.

In the caverns there was no way to tell how much time had passed and Ashes busied himself with sharpening his blades gathering wood and caring for China. When he had finished carrying in the last load of firewood Ashes dug out his currying brush, it was old and the bristles were falling out but it did the job. He always loved brushing his own horses it relaxed him as much as it seemed to the horses and it gave him time to think.

It had only been a day's ride from the oasis before they had run into the storm and at least two days more to Summer if they run into no more delays. He was still not sure how to handle the reunion or what kind of welcome he would get.

He loved Summer he had never stopped loving Summer, and from what the gem had shown him she felt the same about him.

But her loving him would not save him from her anger about him leaving her twenty years ago. He had done it for what he thought was in her best interest. But it was doubtful she would feel the same way he was just as likely to get a knee to the groin when she saw him as a hug. Brushing the sand and dried sweat from China's flank Ashes noticed a sore on the stallion's back where the sand had worked its way under the saddle.

Inspecting it closely he decided it was not bad enough yet to cause any serious problems but he would have to watch it closely, infection could spread quickly and a sick or weak horse could cost a man his life. He brushed around the sore gently before opening the water bottle again and poured a stream of the cold water onto the sore cleaning it out with a corner of his last shirt.

"Going to be running around naked if this keeps up", Ashes muttered. Looking at the sore again after he cleaned it he decided it would be best to walk the next few days to give it time to heal. It had nothing to do with the fact he still was not sure what he was going to say to Summer when he saw her again.

"Yeah, keep telling yourself that" he muttered. When he finished brushing the horse he decided to gather more firewood being old and dry the wood burned quickly. But the forest of strange sticks poking above the cave floor gave him plenty of fuel for the fire. Not for the first time he wondered how it had gotten like that the spikes sticking through the cave floor reminded him of a miniature woodland forest.

The wood broke easily at ground level when he pushed on it with a boot breaking off with a loud snap that echoed off the far cave walls. In no time at all he had gathered a large armload of wood and headed back to camp.

As he neared the camp he heard a loud thump and a satisfied grunt coming from the other side of the fire, he didn't even have to look to know the source. The shadowy outline of an upside down horse and the legs waving in the air confirmed his suspicions as China flipped from one side to the other in a happy roll.

"That's it, horse. Work the dirt in good, it's not like I just cleaned you up or anything." Shoving himself to his hooves and giving himself a last good shake to fling off the sand China looked over at Ashes with a smug look.

"Yeah, I know," the look said, "You're mad, but you will get over it." Glaring at the horse Ashes started stacking the wood by the fire putting the last piece on the stack he stopped surprised, staring hard at the wood he turned it over in his hands to see it better in the light of the fire. What he had thought to be spider webs or dried moss in the cave darkness was dried leaves Ashes studied the log a minute longer before looking out at the spikes sticking above the cave floor, treetops they were treetops there was no denying it the entire cavern had been at one time filled with trees. Before he had time to ponder the meaning of this new discovery China's battle scream echoed off the cavern walls.

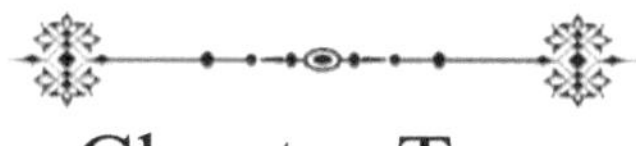

Chapter Two
Serpent Poison

Dropping the log and drawing his sword he spun around he had no idea who or what their enemy was but one thing he knew for sure was that there was little that could upset the stallion like that. Ashes saw the stallion on the other side of the fire rearing and striking at something on the ground, but with the fire between them he could not see what the stallion was fighting.

Running around the fire he almost wished had hadn't, except where they were standing and the fire itself the whole ground was covered with huge serpentine bodies twisting and slithering over each other the get to them.

Ashes jumped back just in time to avoid a lightning fast strike from the nearest one, landing off balance he steadied himself against China's flank before returning to the fight taking a backhanded swing at the closest of the snakes. The blade sliced through the air where the savage head had been a heartbeat ago.

Damn!

Even for snakes these things are fast, He thought. China shot forward in a blurring lunge grabbing one of the snakes that had moved to slow in his teeth. The stallion shook his head back and forth violently before releasing the snake flinging it against a large boulder, the snake struck the hard rock face before falling to the ground limp.

Another snake stuck at Ashes' ankle the glistening fangs glancing off the heavy leather off his boot. Ashes managed to bring his foot down on the scaly head trapping it long enough for him to finish the job with a thrust of his sword. The body wiggled violently in the sand even without its head. Ashes jerked his foot back staring in surprise as he recognized this particular breed of snake -- dragon serpents!

Dragon serpents were given their name for the shape of their head they truly looked like the creatures of Lohr that they were named after. That and their size and mouths full of razor-sharp teeth.

They were a very deadly enemy.

But the most concerning thing about them was their venom there was none more deadly, one bite from one of these creatures and a man would be dead before he hit the ground. Ashes scanned the cavern trying to find a way out past these deadly snakes, he would figure out where they came from and how they got here later.

Another snake far bigger than the first one struck at Ashes flipping his sword in his hand he flung it at the serpent as it coiled for another strike. The blade spun once in the air before striking the snake between the eyes as it struck out at him again, the serpent fell into the sea of squirming bodies.

China let out a squeal of anger and pain Ashes spun around in time to see the big horse bring his hoof down on a snake head. Ashes blood turned cold though when he saw the fang marks in the horse's fetlock. They had to end this now! He was not sure how fast the venom would work on a horse, especially one as big and strong as China but the longer this fight went on the less chance the horse had.

Grabbing up the supply bag off the ground he dumped the contents out spotting what he was looking for the oil!

There was no time for subtlety.

Ashes brought his boot down hard on the bottleneck. The bottleneck broke under his boot when he stomped grabbing the bottle up he spun in place shaking the oil on the snakes using the momentum from his spin he knocked the burning wood from the fire onto the oil-soaked snakes. The oil caught more quickly than Ashes expected jumping from one snake to the next as they bumped into each other trying to flee the flames.

Ashes felt a moment of pity for the serpents it was not something he enjoyed doing had there been any other way he would have used it, but China's life was on the line and if despite all his veiled threats otherwise, his life would be very lonely without his large friend. The cavern filled with the stench of burnt flesh and wood smoke as the snakes disappeared in the darkness. Ashes hardly noticed them as he kneeled down to examine China's leg.

The logs from the fire were scattered across the floor but some still burned enough to throw off enough light for him to see China was in trouble already. The stallion was hanging his head and blowing hard through wide nostrils. Ashes had very little time he kept a small bag of medical supplies with him, but he had nothing on hand for a snake bite it was not something a mercenary had to deal with very often.

Thinking hard he searched through the supplies he had the most important thing right now was keeping the poison from spreading the bite was low on the leg there was not much chance that the fangs had struck a vein if it had the poison would have already spread through the horse's body and there would be no saving his friend. Still, China's life was in danger not even a horse as strong as the stallion could beat the dragons' serpents' venom without help.

Grabbing up a small coil of rope he looped it just above China's knee and tied it leaving enough room to slip a stout branch threw twisting the branch he tightened the rope tight cutting off the blood flow from the already swollen fetlock. China's ears flicked in annoyance but he kept his leg still sensing that Ashes was trying to help him.

Ashes drew his boot dagger and made a quick slice across the bite marks careful not to cut the tendons running through fetlock. Blood spurted around the blade staining the cave floor. Ashes jerked back staring in the dim light he could see the vile yellow venom oozing out of the wound, he knew better than to try to suck the poison out like he had heard of men doing in the past.

Even with a snake less venomous than a dragon serpent that would be a foolish thing to do, men had died doing such a thing. Still, the poison had to be drawn out as much as possible he had spent a lot of time in the Roian Wars listening to the old healer in between battles surely the old man had said something about such things in his stories. Yes, yes! There had been a time when he spoke of a poultice he had made from dirt and plants to draw poison out!

Flipping his shield over he gathered up some ashes from the fire mixing it in with the soft dirt on the cave floor untying the water bottle again, he poured a steady stream of water into the mix, stirring it till he had a thick paste. He did not have any of the plants that the healer had spoken of but he did have several setas left.

Dumping the bag out, he grabbed up the biggest of them and spotting a group of large rocks sitting nearby he placed the fruit on a large one with a flat surface bringing a smaller rock down hard on it, he ground the fruit into a gooey mush that he mixed into the muddy paste of dirt and ash.

The resulting mix was far from appealing and Ashes had a moment of doubt as to whether or not it would be a good idea to put such a mess on an open wound but he had few choices. If this did not work China would die a slow painful death, and he was not about to let that happen. If he failed in stopping the poison from spreading he would use his sword to give the horse a painless death before he let him suffer and hope that the stallion would forgive him when they met in the afterlife.

Taking a hand full of the gooey mix he worked it into the wound making sure he left none uncovered. Then he pulled out his extra shirt again and wrapped it tightly around the leg before undoing the tourniquet. China lifted his leg starring at the strange thing wrapped around it then pawed the ground annoyed. "Stop that!" Ashes snapped, "The more you get worked up the faster the poison spreads you need to calm down." Looking down at the remaining setas, Ashes grunted the most potent wine known was made from Setas very rare and very valuable because it took so long for the fruit to ferment and to brew the wine otherwise you got a foul-tasting drink a drunk man could not gag down.

Dumping the remaining poultice of mud and fruit onto a rock to use later, Ashes threw the scattered pieces of firewood into a pile again and fanned the embers he was quickly rewarded with a bright flame lapping hungrily at the wood.

Working quickly he put the rest of the fruits in the shield and once more pounded the fruits into a paste stopping every few minutes to mix in water from the water bag then sat the shield with the mix on to the hot fire. After what seemed like an eternity the mixture began to boil.

China's breathing was still harsh but it did not seem to be getting worse. Hopefully, if he acted in time, with the seta juice and could get the horse to drink it would relax him and slow his heartbeat slowing down Any Venom that might still be in his blood. Using his boot He pushed the shield of the hot embers and carefully poured some of the remaining water in the boiling goo to cool it.

If they were careful, there was enough water left to last a day, finding more water would have to be his first priority if they were to make it much further. The water not only cooled the goo it thinned it as well, sticking a finger in the mix he tasted it. It had a different strong alcoholic taste to it, good if he could get the horse to drink if he was sure it would do the job. Stripping off his shirt and again pulling out his extra one to protect his hands from the heat he lifted the hot shield to the horse's muzzle.

China took a half-hearted sniff at the shield and its contents then turned his head away, shifting his weight Ashes moved around the hot embers trying not to spill the cavern-made brew as he tried to keep shield under the horse's nose.

It took several minutes and more than one threat from the man but finally, the stud lowered his head enough to take a questioning sip of the sticky mess. Ashes watched the horse's neck intently for the tell-tale jerk that would let him know that the horse was swallowing. Feeling a moment of relief when China swallowed. Ashes' biggest fear had been whether or not he could get the horse to drink the ghastly mess. If it did not take too long to take effect the horse might make it.

Once he started to drink China surprised Ashes' by not stopping till he drained the shield of its contents. "Huh, you might have saved me a taste." Ashes muttered, even if he could talk, the horse would not have been able to do so clearly. It was obvious that the wine was having its effect. Swaying back and forth on his hooves the horse took two slow clumpy steps before folding his hind legs and ungracefully dropping his rump to the ground with a loud thump, the rest of his body quickly followed.

The cavern was filled with the sound of a soft rumbling snore as he dropped into a deep sleep. The sight and sound was reassuring but the horse was not out of danger, it would take several days for his body to fight off the reaming poison that was still in his system. But still, Ashes started to relax at least about this problem, "One thing at a time," he told himself, "Once China is out of danger then we will worry about the rest."

Scraping what was left of the setas goo out of the bottom of the shield he mixed it with the remaining mix from earlier and after unwrapping the makeshift bandage the horse leg he brushed off the drying paste from earlier and applied a fresh layer, the seta juice would help draw the poison and help with the swelling after rewrapping the horse's leg he banked the fire and put the remaining supplies back in the supply bags before throwing any of the dead snake bodies he could find as far out in the cavern as he could.

Strange when he thought about it that they had not tried to attack again, Dragon serpents were fierce predators from what he had heard of them they did not quite after an attack till they made a kill or were killed themselves.

Still, there was no telling with snakes, he was tempted to sneak back to the cave opening to see if the storm had stopped, but he did not want to leave the horse unguarded. It would not make any difference now anyway even if it had, China would not be able to travel for a day or two and he was not going to leave his friend behind. Using his saddle as a chair he stared intently into the darkness of the cavern the fire flames threw dancing lights on the far walls like a living thing, watching them Ashes suddenly jerked alert, two of the lights were unmoving, steady and intent something was watching them!

In an instant Ashes was on his feet, putting himself between the slumbering horse and the newcomer. "Who are you? What do you want?" Only silence answered him. Cursing, he charged the glowing orbs, he'd had enough of this place! The eyes watched his charge unconcerned as his attack was suddenly stopped when his foot found one of the hidden spikes sticking above the cavern floor sending him sliding ungracefully across the hard ground. Angry and embarrassed he pushed himself to his feet, the fall had not helped his mood pushed past anger now he charged the glowing orbs again.

"You should not be here, leave before you are taken like the others, *leave now!*" the voice echoed off the walls of the cavern but Ashes got the feeling that the voice did not belong to the glaring eyes seemingly floating in the darkness, shaking off the dizziness from his fall he cursed his own clumsiness as he pushed even faster toward the thing taunting him. A heavy weight slammed into his chest sending him stumbling backwards before falling again into the forest of spikes that littered the cave floor.

Sharp pain shot through his leg, looking down he saw a bloody spike sticking like a wooden tooth through his calf, blood quickly started to pool under the wound but his attacker gave him no time to worry about how bad he was hurt as the weight on his chest grew ever more Forcing the air out of his lungs "No!"

He was not going to die like this!

Snarling, he swung wildly with his sword trying to free himself. But his sword passed through the air above him meeting no resistance.

Struggling under the weight he tried to find the leverage to free himself when a hot breath struck his face filling the air with a stench that burned his eyes. "What are you going to do now little fool? You are as helpless as all the other fools who dared try to take what is mine."

The pressure on his chest grew, even more, forcing the last of the air out of his lungs. Ashes made one last desperate attempt to free himself from his attacker but neither his sword nor his fist found an opponent.

His vision started to blur as he fought to stop from losing consciousness. His vision was starting to fade when he heard a furious whinny and razor-sharp hooves struck at the glowing orbs now just above his head.

China?

His friend had heard the fight and somehow found the strength to come to his rescue, the last thing he heard before he lost consciousness was an inhuman shriek

An echoing voice pulled him back to consciousness. "I know you are hurt, child, but there is no time to rest the Dark Ankra will not stay away for long we must go." The voice was female, deep, and strangely wispy but there was no doubt that the speaker was a female.

His ribs protested as he sat up, not broken thankfully but still sore, the blood covered spike held his calf fast like a living thing, stealing himself he put both hands palm down on the ground and jerked his trapped leg upward quickly freeing it, sending a spray of blood on the dirt floor.

Tearing a strip off the bottom of his pants, he made a makeshift bandage to stop the flow of blood. It would have to be good enough for now, there were other matters that were more important.

Looking around he tried to find his rescuer as far as he could tell he was alone the only sign of life was the light from his own fire dancing on the far cavern wall. He was just about to think that he had imagined the voice and its owner when he heard it again.

A deep and almost musical voice echoing not off the cavern walls but in his head. "Can you walk? Use a stick to help you if you must but we cannot stay here we must hurry we need to go -- we do not have much time!"

Turning a slow circle Ashes searched the darkness, "Where are you? I can't follow you if I can't see you."

"Behind you", came the answer, turning quickly he stared hard at the bleakness in front of him nothing, nothing but rocks, darkness and shadows, enough of this foolishness angrily he started to draw his sword.

"Stay your hand child, I mean you no harm and your weapon would do you no good to those that dwell here that do."

Unconvinced, he held the sword at ready, "Then show yourself, if you mean no ill why hide?"

Laughter echoed in his head "I am not hiding child, I am where I said I would be I am just not what you thought I would be." A misty shape stepped out from between two of the boulders to stand in front of him "Do you see me now child?"

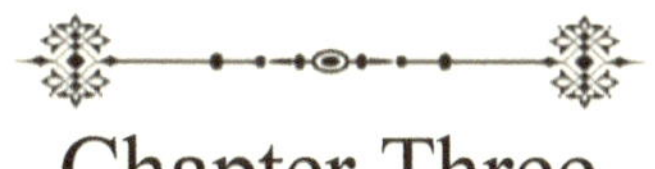

Chapter Three
A Tail of Myths and Shadows

Ashes Stared at the newcomer in Surprise, he was expecting to see a female but not a mare especially one who could "talk". Again he heard the echoing laughter in his head, 'As I said not what you expected am I child?"

The shock passed quickly, studying the mare he saw she was far from a normal horse aside from talking, her mane and tail seemed to be blowing in a wind far stronger than the faint breeze that came from the cavern depths and he was still not sure if it was a trick from the far off fire light, but her outline seemed to be moving almost like clouds racing across a stormy sky what held his attention the most was her eyes large and beautiful, staring into them he could swear he could see lighting dancing in them, that had to be the fire light reflecting off them Lately I have run into a lot of strange things, he thought why not a talking horse? "You said that thing was a Dark Ankra? I never heard of them before, what are they and how do you kill them?" he asked warily

The mare shook her mane snorting "You can't, At least not here in this place, the best we can do is drive them off, but that one will return and not alone we must be as far away as possible when they do. Come now lean on me for support if you must but hurry."

Ashes grimaced as he limped toward the mare, after lifting her head to scan the darkness of the cavern she bunched her hindquarters and jumped the last few rocks between them turning her flank to him letting him Put an arm across her withers, "Thanks but if we are in such a hurry, wouldn't it be faster if I rode you?" he ask.

The mare cocked an eye at him, "If there was not the need, I would not allow this we both risk much by this but that is something you cannot yet understand and the need is great we have little choice."

Grunting as he tried to keep up with the mare and keep as much weight as possible off his hurt leg "You still have not answered my question, what are these things and why have they attacked us? Is this their lair?"

Her answer echoed softly in his head, "The Dark Arnka are servants of Molder a very evil and powerful creature not of this world he would destroy every living thing on this and every world if he had his way. There is much you need to know but not now. Here sit and rest I must wake the stallion."

Ashes looked around in surprise he hadn't even realized that they had arrived at the camp. Sliding his arm off the mare he found a large rock to sit on as he inspected his hurt leg. The wound was clean passing through the thick muscle on the back of his leg just missing the bone. He tore another strip of cloth of his pants leg wetting it with some of the remaining water gingerly cleaning the wound before retiring the bandage.

As he was tying the last knot on the bandage he heard an excited snort followed by the stallions' whinny no doubt about it China was awake and had no trouble recognizing that this new horse was a mare, stepping high he pranced around the mare arching his powerful neck seemingly forgetting about his own injury, Every man's dream Ashes thought to wake up with a pretty female next to him, he could not help laughing, "My friend I don't think you could handle this one"

As if to prove his point the mare reared up to strike out with a hoof at a boulder next to the stallion the strike sent sparks flying through the air like lightning bolts and sent a rolling echo across the cavern like distant thunder, "ENOUGH!" The angry whinny echoing in Ashes head was nothing like the soft-spoken words before and had their intended effect. China stopped his prancing and backed away from the mare cowered, Ashes had never seen him like that nothing had ever intimidated his horse.

"Mind your manners colt there is no time for this foolishness," Turning to Ashes she went on. "He is still weak but he will be able to carry you and your weapons nothing else you will have to leave you saddle and supplies here." She went on quickly before he could protest. "You will not be needing them it is not a long journey to where we are going and I can show you where to find food and water."

The mare eyes softened.

"I know I am asking a lot of your child and your colt but please you must trust me there is a great deal more at stake than you know much is happening and you have a great part to play in it. Now please hurry, follow me."

After sliding the bridle over China's head Ashes pulled himself up onto the strong back and turned the horse to follow the strange mare. Nudging the horse's flank to catch up, "Why are we going this way, isn't the cave entrance we came through is the other way?" he asks

"The storm buried the entire ridge the only way for you to get out now is on the other side of the caverns, as I said it is not very far maybe a day's travel as long as we keep our rest short." flicking her ears she added "I know you both are hurt so if you need to rest longer we will but please remember what I said we are racing time."

"You ask us to trust you and we will." he told her, "But can you at least tell us what is happening? It would make it a little easier to play my part if I knew what it was. All I know for sure is we are riding through a dark cave full of things that want to kill us for reasons I don't know following a talking horse, I don't even know your name if you have one!"

The mare turned an amused eye on him, "I will tell you my name soon enough it is not important right now, and as for the other, animals talk all the time child you just have to learn to listen to them, a dog will tell his master when there is danger or when it is just happy, a cat will do so as well, cow, bears, pigs, birds, all animals talk child but humans have grown so used to their own ways they have lost the ability to understand, I pity them for that. The stallion you are riding now speaks to you every day, his nicker of greeting, his snort of amusement, the joy in his eyes when he has carried you safely through a battle you are his life child he would die under you if you ask never forget that."

Looking down at China Ashes felt a pang of guilt, remembering the oasis and the gem, he still was not sure if what had happened had been a dream. China had done just that in that other place, killed by a madman's spear in a desperate battle to save a kingdom. He would never forget the feeling seeing his friend dying not being able to do anything about it. "I would die myself before I let that happen he is far more than just a horse."

"You are a good man Child but sometimes there are things that happen we have no control over. Only God knows what our tomorrows will bring, we must trust in him that he will always be with us to help us through them." A great sorrow showed in her eyes as the mare turned her attention back to the trial ahead.

"You keep calling me a child," He told her, "It has been a long time since I was a child."

"I mean no insult or disrespect." She answered him her eyes still focused on the trail ahead. "How old are you, child? Forty-Three is it not?" Ashes stared at her in silence he could not believe that that was just a guess, who was this mare? Turning her head to look at him she went on, "You have seen forty-three summers have you not? And the stallion what? Eight?" She let out a soft whinny of laughter as she turned her eyes back to the trial. "Even if it was ten times that or a hundred you would still be a child to me, but if it puts you at ease, I will call you by your given name Ashes son of Poppy the swift and Sparkla the kind is that not right?"

Reining China in Ashes snapped, "You know a lot about me but you still have not even told me your name, we go no further till you do!"

The strange mare never even broke stride, "I think we do child as I said we have no time for foolishness." Glancing back at China she let out a long soft nicker the studs ears flicked forward than without warning he grabbed the bit in his teeth and trotted to catch up with her.

Glaring down at the stud "traitor" he growled half-heartedly, looking over at the mare he ask, "What did you say to him? That is the first time in years he has done something like that"

"I told him the truth" came the soft voice in his head, "I told him that the more time we waste here the greater the risk to your life." Sighing the mare went on, "You are right to be suspicious child. Ashes!" She hurriedly corrected herself, "In this place especially, I will tell you all that I can but I cannot tell you all that you wish to know right now, that is for another to do."

She turned pleading eyes on him, "But understand that there are forces of great evil at work and even now they are watching and listening to us, they wait for a time to strike and I can only protect you for so long here. And you both are far more important to what is coming than you know now please no more delays we must hurry!" Turning back to the trail she led the way thru the darkness at a fast trot with China and Ashes beside her.

For the next hour, they rode in silence finally he ventured, "What can you tell us about what is happening?"

For several minutes she was silent he was about to repeat his question when she answered, "First tell me this child, what do you know about this land?"

"You mean the desert?" at her nod of assessment he went on, "There are a lot of tales, some say it is cursed, Some say it is haunted, But the one thing that everyone agrees on is that it is very dangerous. Few men will try to cross it unless they have no choice most men will go around.

There are stories of an army of a thousand men that tried to cross about fifty years ago they were never seen again. Searchers found their mounts and supplies, but the men were nowhere to be found. But that was before my time, what I know for sure is that it never stays the same. Maps are useless and landmarks can't be trusted. Makes it damn hard to tell where you are going or where you have been. I have crossed it going on three times now, by what I thought was the same route, and nothing is ever the same."

"Never the same." Came the sad reply in his head.

Ashes stared at her, were there tears in her eyes? Or was it a trick of the light? Sighing she went on, " There was a time young one when this cavern and all the lands around it were mountains and forest as far you could see, the trail we follow now was cut by a great river over two miles wide, herds of deer and elk in the hundreds grazed the valleys. It was a place of such bounty that even in the harshest winter, nothing, and no one went hungry. The kingdom of Brutus-hay!"

Ashes stared at her in disbelief, "Brutus-hay?!" he ask, "You expect me to believe that Brutus-hay really existed? Every child's mother has told them tales of Brutus-hay it is a child's fantasy nothing more!"

"I forgive you your insult child because you know no better, but I do not lie, soon very soon you will understand what once was can be again." Stopping suddenly she jerked her head up her nostrils wide and her ears alert. Snorting loudly she slapped China with her tail, "Run!" Her voice echoed loudly in their heads "Their coming follow me quickly, Run!"...

Ashes let the reins go slack giving the horse his head as he fell in behind the mare trusting her to lead the way as they raced through the darkness the thunder of hooves echoing off the far off walls.

Looking over her shoulder the mare made a series of snorts at the stallion China's ears flicked forward as he listened intently. Looking back Ashes tried to spot their pursuers nothing but darkness, wait! Staring hard he could just make out the dim glow of eyes their unseen owners closing the gap between them. "We can't run forever!" he yelled, "We have to fight them here!"

The mare slowed her pace enough to let them come alongside her. "Listen to me child, there are too many of them, they are no threat to me it is you they are after. I will hold them off here long enough for you to get away. In just under a mile the tunnel splits you need to take the smaller of the two it will lead you out of these lands, I already told the stallion he knows what he must do. As I said I will hold these off but there are many more and they will follow you." The voice grew stern as she glared at him.

"Do not try to fight them in this place, you will lose! And much will be lost because of it. They can leave the caverns I cannot, at least not yet, but to do so they have to take a body of flesh and blood then they can be hurt and killed, even so it would be foolishness to try to fight them unless you have no choice, there are too many. Listen closely child as soon as you reach the end of the tunnel head west into the sun half a day's ride you will find allies and help."

Before he could ask any of the hundreds of questions that were swirling in his head she went on. "Trust me, child, you will understand everything soon enough." Sliding to a stop she spun to face their pursuers. "When you see Buck give him a message for me, tell him, what once was can be again but for it to be so first he must seek forgiveness from the one who was hurt the most by his mistake."

Grabbing up the reins he pulled hard on them China slowed but did not stop. "Wait!" he yelled over his shoulder, "Who is Buck? And how can I give him your message if I don't even know your name!"

The darkness quickly swallowed her up as China continued his headlong run but the echoing voice in his head was still strong, "Well he knows who I am child but you can call me what men of this world have called me for millennia, I am Stormracer!"

"Stormracer!" Ashes repeated the name in his mind, a name that men still spoke today though most agreed that there never was such thing as a spirit horse that ran through the clouds controlling the weather, a child's tale, Stormracer was a myth a tale wasn't it? "Yea" he thought, "Just like Bruits -hay and the Dark Arnka and jewels that granted wishes…." He let the thought trail off...

China swerved suddenly jerking him out of his thoughts, they were racing down the narrow tunnel and for the first time in days the sunlight struck his face as the horse shot out of the cave mouth. After the darkness of the caverns the sunlight was almost overwhelming forcing them to stop long enough to give their eyes time to adjust rather than risk a broken leg. Shading his eyes with his hand he scanned the landscape checking to see if they had been followed and to get his bearings.

The tunnel had let them out in a long valley with tall dunes cresting on both sides of the cave mouth the only mar on the bleak landscape. Still, it was a vast improvement over the darkness of the caverns and there was no sign of pursuit, at least not yet, maybe the mare had been wrong about that. He heard the snarl before he even finished the thought the grey-black shapes seemed to grow out of the dunes themselves as the Dark Arnka closed in from all sides.

China leaped forward sending a spray of sand behind the as he bowled over the ones trying to block their path, bones broke loudly as he left a trail of bodies in his wake. Letting the reins go slack Ashes drew his sword taking a backhand swing he sliced through the neck of one that had avoided the stallions charge and tried to sink its fangs into the horse back leg.

The Dark Arnka gave chase but was starting to fall behind, he was just starting to think that they were going to get away when without a fight when China's leg sunk deep into a hidden sinkhole. Sending the horse tumbling head over heels into the sand, Ashes flew over the horses head and slammed hard into the side of a dune

Spitting out a mouth full of sand he shoved himself to his feet, grabbing up his sword he spun around looking for China. The horse was already on his hooves ready for battle he was favoring his left foreleg but it did not seem to be broken. He had no time to check for sure as the air was filled with inhuman shrieks and the Dark Arnka was on them.

The Dark Arnka was like nothing he had ever seen before, they resembled the drawings he had saw in the roman high priest prayer chambers years ago. Not animal and not human, they ran on all four legs like a deformed dog but stood on their hind legs like a bear to do battle. The thing was they looked nothing like bears or dogs, the best way he could think of to describe one if he had to was a very ugly cross between a chimp and rat. Having a chimp like face with over muscled jaws and mouths with way too many teeth combined with a hairless rat like body ending with a whip like tale full of razor sharp barbs.

A warhorse knows what is expected of it, working with their rider as a team, and China was one of the best warhorses Ashes had ever seen. Even with only three good legs, the stallion struck with lightning speed with both hooves and teeth making his way back to his rider's side. Striking out savagely at a dark shape leaping at them trying to give the man time to climb on to his back, but even as one fell under his hooves another took its place.

Rearing on his hind legs he came down with all his weight on the backs of two Dark Arnka who were trying to sneak up on his rider. The blow broke both of his targets backs the bodies sliding in the loose sand throwing him off balance, giving another of the enemy the opening it needed.

Sinking its teeth into the horse's back leg and pulling it out from under him as he tried to get his balance. The stallion kicked out hard freeing his back leg but could not get his hooves back under him before several more were on top of him with a whiny of rage he was pulled over on his side.

Ashes was covered in foul smelling blood several Dark Arnka bodies lay scattered around his feet. Backing slowly he stood sword ready watching warily as he found himself facing four of the creatures coming at him in a snarling half circle.

He could sense the fight going on behind him and knew that China needed help, swinging his sword in a wide one handed arch he spun quickly drawing a dagger from his belt he hurled it at a dark shape lunging for the horses exposed belly. Then using the momentum from the spin he jumped over the horse putting all the power he could into a savage swing driving their enemy back long enough for the stallion to get his hooves back under him.

China shoved himself to his feet furious, he wanted nothing more than to make these foul things pay for this attack but countless battles had taught him to know when things were going badly for them, as much as he hated it he knew that their only chance was to outrun these disgusting things. Ducking his head low he spun around with a hard kick sending the closest ones flying and clearing a path for them to get away. Understanding what the horse was doing Ashes threw an arm around the powerful neck and jumped onto the broad back, before the Dark Arnka had a chance to react the stallion charged threw the resulting gap in the circle and was racing away.

Leaning low against the racing horses neck Ashes took a second to evaluate their chances, both of them were hurt but not too bad, not yet. The biggest worry he had was that any of the dragon-serpent venoms still in China's blood would weaken the horse enough that any injuries even small one would kill him.

His friends breathing was already growing harsher than it would normally be in such a fight, they had to find a way to end this now!

The Dark Arnka gave chase pursuing them down the length of the valley, Ashes had not carried a bow in many years, he regretted that now, he had used the last of his daggers in the previous fight. All he had left was his sword and his long knife he had a feeling that he would need both if they were to have any chance of surviving another fight with these things.

And after leaving the supply bags back in the caverns he didn't even have anything to throw in the path of these things to distract them. "Damn!" he thought bitterly the only thing he could throw at them right now was insults.

The stallion slowed his pace and blew out loudly pulling him out of his thoughts, looking ahead he could see the dark shapes running down the dunes in their direction. At first glance they looked like more Dark Arnka, but as they drew closer he could see they were something else more familiar, larger and far more deadly. Ashes felt a cold knot in his gut, he was far from a coward but also not a fool, and there was no way the two of them was going to win this battle not so badly outnumbered.

China seemed to agree with him coming to a stop saving all his strength to take as many of the foe as he could with him in their final battle. The only question was what was going to reach them first, the Dark Arnka or the Desert cats?

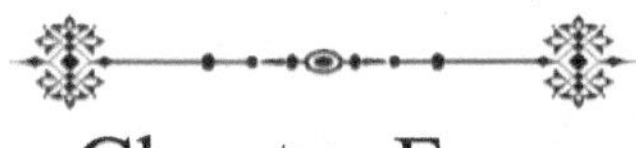

Chapter Four
A Desert Of Secrets

Ashes was both relieved and insulted as the Desert cats ignored them streaking by on both sides in a headlong charge at the Dark Arnka. Numbers were on the Dark Arnka side but the Desert cats did not seem to care it was clear from the start who the victors of this battle were going to be. They hit the Dark Arnka at a dead run leaving a trail of bloody and torn bodies in their wake in all his life he had never seen a more one-sided battle he almost felt sorry for the Dark Arnka.....almost.

His first instinct had been to help the Desert cats, but it was clear that they did not need his help, in fact, the battle was coming to an end as he watched the Dark Arnka that still could were in a full retreat leaving most of their number behind. Grateful for the Desert cats help but not willing to test his luck he nudged China in the side keeping a wary eye on the Desert cats trying not to draw attention to themselves. The Desert cats were intent on their fleeing foe now but that could change very quickly, understanding the danger China turned away slowly from the big cats and started back down the desert trail.

"You have nothing to fear from them, they mean you no harm if they had you would have known it by know...and you would be dead." The voice startled Ashes twisting around to find its owner he felt a sharp pain in his side, looking down he saw his shirt and pants leg soaked in blood the jagged end of a Dark Arnka tail spike buried deep in his side. For a second he was unsure how then he remembered jumping across China in the last battle when he had sliced the Dark Arnka he had just dodged a full hit by the creatures tail getting only a glancing blow. He had thought nothing of it at the time, he had felt the blow but there was no pain. That was until now. "Just great," he muttered, "My last shirt." Then the desert hit him in the face.

The pain in his side woke him, blinking his eyes he tried to remember where he was and how he got there. The last thing he could remember was hearing the strange voice and the Desert cats...China! Where was his friend? His side protested as he sat up quickly looking around he realized he had no idea where he was at or how he got here. The bed and room he was in at one time been very beautiful with a large fountain sitting in the middle of the room with paintings and sculptures lining the walls, he could not help but be impressed to think of what it must have looked like at one time, there would be time to figure such things out later.

He had to find China, his head throbbed as he sat the rest of the way up and swung his feet to the floor. Two things became very clear as he shoved himself to his feet one, he was not wearing any clothes and two he should have waited a few more seconds before he tried to stand. That was made very clear as he fell ungracefully face first onto the floor. Cursing his clumsiness for what seemed like the tenth time that day he rolled over onto his back, just as the door opened and a stranger entered carrying a tray full of strange smelling liquids and bandages.

A look of alarm flashed on the man's face, "Here let me help you or you will reopen your wounds", Sitting the tray on the table next to the bed he reached down sliding his arms under Ashes back and legs and lifted him off the floor and back onto the bed. Ashes was impressed he was not a small man but this stranger had lifted him easily.

"Don't worry you are among friends now if you will let me I need to redress your wounds." reaching down he started unwrapping the bloody bandage.

"Where am I and where is my horse?" Ashes demanded

"Your horse is safe and resting in the stables next to this building he is as strong as he is loyal and stubborn, we had a very hard time getting him to let us near you to help. As soon as I am done cleaning your wounds I will take you to him it might help you both, you will not be able to walk on your own just yet I think, so you are going to have lean on me." Glancing up from his work he added, "You are both very lucky to be alive a shadow stalkers venom is normally deadly you are the only man I have known to survive a strike from one, and if I am not mistaken that is a dragon serpent's bite on the stallion's leg, I have never known anything to survive one of their bites.

He is a very strong horse as you seem to be a very strong man. But regardless of how strong you are you both need to rest and let yourselves heal or you will soon run out of luck." after he finished rewrapping the wound on Ashes side he started on his leg, Ashes flinched as the crusted bandage was pulled away from his swollen calf.

As he was inspecting the wound a large shape silently came through the doorway a smile tugged on the corners of the strangers face. "That is one of your rescuers meet Cinnamon." Ashes had no trouble recognizing the animal as one of the Desert cats, a large female who's graying face and whiskers did not seem to fit the large heavily muscled body,

"The other four who came to your aide are her cubs, she showed up pregnant some time ago and gave birth in the garden they have lived here ever since only leaving to hunt like they were when they heard your battle with the shadow stalkers."

Ashes studied the big cat, the sun shining thru the window light up the highlights on her sleek brown pelt, making it easy to see how she had gotten her name her cinnamon brown fur seemed to glow in the dim light. Padding over to stand next to him she studied him with unsettling intensity before lifting her head to let out a soft chirping grunt.

From some were on the other side of the door came an answering call as its owner padded through the doorway another Desert cat younger and bigger than the old female, three more followed closely behind making the room seem suddenly much smaller. One by one the big cats settled around the room studying him. Two male and two female as best as he could guess, they all varied in color and size but they all had one thing in common, they all had the swollen bellies and contented look of having just feed.

"Their curious about you, we do not get many strangers and you are stranger than most," Finished cleaning the wound he started re-bandaging the leg, As I said meet your rescuers the old girl you know, the two-tone tabby female sitting next to her is Cactus Jack" hearing her name the she-cat rose to her paws and padded over to the speaker fondly rubbing her body against him reaching down he stroked the big head as he went on.

"The orange tabby male next to your bed is Bane and the White female next to him is Mulberry." Walking over to the biggest and by far the heaviest of the big cats he squatted down and lay his arm affectionately across its neck. "And this big boy is Sugar Britches."

Ashes had been listening quietly as the stranger had told him the big cat's names but he could not help laughing "Sugar Britches? It is a good thing he cannot understand you old man I don't think he would be too happy with that name."

Scratching between the big animal's ears the stranger chuckled "You insult them they are far more intelligent than you think, as I said they were born in the garden I named them all from plants growing in the garden, I am not very imaginative when it comes to such things."

Still smiling Ashes jerked a thump in the big grey's direction "I don't know much about garden plants but I am pretty sure there are none named Sugar Britches" As he was talking the big cat rolled over on his side trapping his human friend under his weight slapping playfully at the man with a velvet paw.

None of the Desert cats was the same color from Mulberry's gleaming white pelt to Cinnamons surgery brown Sugar Britches was no difference going from a dark grey head blending into a lighter grey towards his hindquarters.

"They seem very fond of you" Ashes observed "I did not think that Desert cats took to humans very well almost every story I have heard about people trying to tame them did not end very well. Even when they were raised from cubs like you said these were, they always revert back to their wild ways."

Putting his hands against the furry side the newcomer gave a futile shove trying to get out from under what was at the moment an oversized kitten Realizing that he had a better chance of moving the castle he let out a resigned sigh. "As I said they were born in the garden I was there when they were born and I was there when they first opened their eyes, they have known me all their lives I think they see me as their father." The last part of his sentence was muted by a huge head as Sugar Britches rubbed a furry cheek across his human friends face.

It was hard to believe that this was the same animal that had been tearing the Dark Arnka limb from limb not long ago. "My friends call me Ashes." he chuckled "You introduced me to all your friends but I have no idea what to call you."

Squirming out from under the big cat the stranger stuck out his hand "My apologies." He muttered glaring at Sugar Britches as he spit out a mouth full of fur, "My manners are rusty I do not get many guests you may call me Buck and welcome to our home." Glancing around embarrassed he added "Such as it is."

Ashes took the offered hand surprised at the strength in the grip. In size and weight Buck was average at best and looked to be at least twenty years older than he was, but the power in his grip and the ease in which he had lifted him off the floor both belied his apparent age, this man would be a very difficult opponent in a fight for any man. "As I said I am called Ashes my horses' name is China and it seems we both are in your debt for saving our lives."

"You owe us nothing," Buck answered him, "We did what any decent person would do no more, you and your horse are both welcome to stay as long as you wish, we do not get many travelers and we do not travel far from these walls ourselves so it would be good to hear any news you wish to share from the world abroad."

"I will be happy to share with you what news I have, but bear in mind most of what I have heard these last few years has been mainly gossip and stories from around campfires in one battle to the next, I can't swear as to how true any of it is…."

A loud whiny interrupted Ashes sitting up stiffly he yelled out the window. "Keep your tail on stud I will there in a minute!"

Walking over to him Buck squatted down and put an arm around his shoulder helping him to stand. "We will talk about the outside world after we have reassured your loud friend that you are still alive."

Putting aside his pride Ashes let himself be helped out the door to the stables he did not want to admit it even to himself that the Dark Arnka venom and the wound to his leg had taken their toll, by the time they reached the stable he was sweating badly and needed a rest. His wounds were not his main worry though he still had the message to give Buck from Stormracer, he was sure that he was the right person, how many people named Buck could there be running around the desert?

But he had an odd feeling that this man would not be happy to hear the news he carried, added to that the message itself---- "Tell Buck what once was, Can be again, But first he must seek forgiveness from the one hurt most by his mistake."--- And to top it off if this was the man that Stormracer had been talking about he would have to be over one thousand years old, the funny thing was, and that was not even the strangest part about the whole thing.

One thing he was sure of though he was going to have to be very careful about how he gave Buck the message.

Like Buck had told him the stables were in the next building as they entered the rich smell of hay and oats filled the air underlined by the heavy scent of horses, it was a smell he had always liked. Even as a mercenary he had spent as much free time as he could working with the horses in the stables.

As it turned out China was not the only horse in the stable, it was a fair size one with about forty stalls on either side of the walkway at the moment only three were in use. China stood in the first stall thrusting his head eagerly over the stall half door nickering a greeting of welcome to his human friend, with Bucks help Ashes limped over to the stallion and scratched the heavily muscled neck the big horse stuck out his head in contentment all but purring. The other two horses stuck their heads out their doors eyeing him curiously.

Nodding at the closest of the two a very pretty brown leopard appaloosa mare Buck told him, "That is Starlight, she wandered in here about ten years ago still wearing a saddle and full supply bags I have no idea what happened to her rider, back tracked her for a full day never found a sign of him or her, a lot of people disappear in this desert, the stallion standing next to her is her colt she dropped him about four months after she got here, kind of a nice surprise I guess, I just thought she was getting fat, his name is Fuzzy."

Ashes had to admit that the stallion fit the name like his dam he was a leopard appaloosa but were his dams coat was covered with brown spots, Fuzzy had a mix of both brown and black spots running up and down his flank, it was the first time he had seen an appaloosa marked in such a way.

On top of the odd coloring, the stallion also boosted a long and heavy coat strange for a desert climate. "His full name is Fuzzy Bunny but I think it embarrasses him so it is just Fuzzy for short." At Ashes questioning look he added " When he was born his hair was even longer than it is now, and he was a small foal I swear I thought she had mated with a mountain heir he could not have looked more like one, so that is why I named him Fuzzy Bunny it just seemed to fit."

"I always said that horses were forgiving animals." Ashes chuckled, "With that name, he must be very forgiving." Laughing Buck slapped him on the back as he opened the door to Starlight stall and started brushing the dried sweat off the mare. Watching him work Ashes debated with himself there was no point in delaying.

Passing on the message that Stormracer had given him he was not sure how Buck would react to the news but he did not think that the man was the "Kill the messenger" type at any rate didn't Stormracer said that things were going to start happening soon?

Still scratching China's neck he tried to act indifferent as he ask "You said those things that attacked us were shadow stalkers?"

Having finished on Starlight's back Buck started on the mare's legs saying absently "Yes, they are common around here, from what I hear from the few other travelers that pass thru here that is not the case everywhere though, I take it you have never come across them before?"

Ashes was looking around for an extra brush finding one on a ledge across from China's stall he started brushing the stallion. "No," he answered, "I never even saw one of those things before a couple of days ago, you called them shadow stalkers someone else I met in the last few days called them by a different name."

Still brushing on Starlight Buck glanced over the mares back at him. "Someone else? I didn't see anyone else when we found you, did the shadow stalkers kill them? If so I am sorry we could not have found you sooner."

Ashes was working on a particularly stubborn spot on the horses back trying to be careful of the sore he had found earlier what seemed like a lifetime ago in reality had only been a couple of days, "The last I saw of her she was still alive I am betting she still is, I don't think that those things could kill her if they tried. Though I am not even sure she is alive at least not in the sense that we are."

Buck had stopped brushing on the mare and was staring at Ashes hard over her back. "She?" He asked "A woman, you met a woman out here, where is she? And what do you mean by she is not alive in the sense we are? I am beginning to think maybe your wounds and the shadow stalkers venom is affecting you more than I thought."

Ashes tapped the brush he was using against the wall to clean out the dried sweat and sand before he answered. "My mind is as clear as ever, so is my memory, and I never said it was a woman that I met, it wasn't."

Squatting down stiffly he started brushing the inside of China's hind leg watching Buck threw the stall boards as he talked "It was a horse, a mare she helped when we first got attacked by those things after a sandstorm trapped us in some caverns not far from here two days ago. And she showed us the way out. And she asked us to deliver a message." Pausing from his brushing he stood returning Bucks stare. "A message to you."

For a long minute both men stared at each other neither man saying anything then Buck broke the silence. "A talking mare you say? And she had a message for me, truly? Tell me then friend before I carry you back up to your bed to sleep of the poisonous effects. What was this imaginary mare's message?"

Uninfected by the other man's words Ashes told him "She said you would know her, her name is Stormracer. And her message was a short one--- Tell Buck that what once was can be again, but first, he must seek forgiveness from the one hurt most by his mistake."

Buck stood unmoving after hearing the message the color drained from his face. Then like a man in a trance he made his way around Starlight and out the stall door as he passed China's stall on his way to the stable entrance. He paused muttering over his shoulder "You seem to be getting your strength back well enough.

I think you can make it back to your room without my help when you are done here, I will check on you in the morning to change your bandages again and bring you your breakfast." Without another word, he headed out of the building with the Desert cats following worriedly behind.

Ashes had not been sure how Buck would react to the message he carried but of all the ways he had imagined this had not been one of them. What had happened in this place? He was more than a little tempted to just ride China as fast as he could away from here but Stormracer had made it plain that he had a part to play in this lands destiny something he did not ask for but somehow he knew that he could not escape it.

After staring thoughtfully at the empty door for a minute he returned back to brushing his horse. He had nothing better to do and it helped him to think. It would be at least two days before he was well enough to ride for any length of time. Even if he did decide to just leave this place to its own fates and continue on his journey to find Summer. As tempting as that thought was he knew that he could never live with himself if he did, it would be too much like running from a fight.

And even though he did not want to admit it he was more than just a little intrigued by what Stormracer had said if this desert had truly, at one time been the kingdom Brutus-Shay and there was even the slightest chance that it could be again. To be a part of that, to see such a place. That would be a memory to cherish in this life as well as the one beyond.

Buck sat in the empty dining hall staring at the far wall and the painting that like him the years had not touched, the paint even though centuries old still shined as brightly as the day that they first touched the canvas.

Ashes words echoed in his head over and over, along with endless questions. How could Stormracer be alive, and if she was why had she not came to him herself with this message? Ask forgiveness from the one hurt most by his mistake?

Had he not begged for forgiveness from the souls of those who lived here? From Stormracer? From God himself? Even this land. Had he not cried a river of tears at his own stupidity? Who was left for him to ask forgiveness of?

"Who else is left for me to ask forgiveness?" Buck said out loud "Tell me what more I can do!! Please, I don't know what you want!! Tell me and I will do it. I am sorry." Lowering his head he repeated, "I am so sorry." Only silence answered him, did you really think anyone was going to answer you? You fool. He thought, this is you're doing! Yours and yours, alone and you deserve your fate to live forever in the wasteland you created."

Standing miserably he turned and started out the doorway of the great hall when a soft voice reached him. "Greetings husband I have missed you."

Spinning around he saw the small women standing in the middle of the room love shining from her eyes. Buck could not stop the tears that flowed down his face or the shuddering sob in his voice as he spoke the name of the women he had not seen in fifteen hundred years "Shilo!"

As she walked towards him he saw that she was wearing the blue blouse and black hunting pants she loved so much, the ones he had given her on her last birthday over a thousand years ago. Only her clothes had changed, in body she had not aged a day from the last time he had seen her leaving the castle so long ago.

"No" She said answering his unasked question, "Unlike you I grew old with time and passed into the next life, I have missed you so much Buck, please you must listen to me. There is much I have to tell you that you must know and we have little time."

The desert sun had already set by the time Ashes left the stables. After he had finished brushing China he started on the other two horses in the stable. Not that they needed it, in fact, they both looked very well taken care of. But they seemed to appreciate it and he had little else to do it kept his mind off the one question that he had no answer for, the one that had been troubling him since he left the oasis. What was he going to say to Summer when he saw her again?

Somehow he did not think that she was just going to welcome into her arms without one hell of a good reason for him leaving her. And he knew the women well enough to know that the "I was just trying to protect you" line as true as it was, would only get him in more trouble. He had faced death too many times to count never once feeling an ounce of fear, so why did the thought of being reunited with the women he loved worry him so much?

He tried to ignore the small voice in the back of his head even though he knew it to be true. "Because without her you are nothing but a mercenary, with nothing to fight for. Only the thought of seeing her again one day has carried you through every battle."

He was feeling somewhat stronger than before but he still had to stop several times to catch his breath as he headed back to the room and was glad no one was around to see him this way, it was bad enough that he had needed Bucks help earlier. And it seemed that if anything the walk back was longer, he was grateful when he reached his room and made a beeline for the bed.

Ashes lowered himself stiffly onto the bed with a grateful grunt, the last few days had taken their toll he didn't even try to fight the heaviness that seemed to drag him into a welcome dreamless sleep.

The room was almost pitch black when something woke him, the sun had surrendered the sky to the nights stars the only light coming from the sliver of an almost hidden moon. A lifetime as a mercenary had sharpened his senses even when he was sleeping. Sitting up half way in the bed he searched the room his hand reaching instantly for his sword when the smell of freshly cooked food reached him.

Sitting up the rest of the way he searched the room for the source of the smell.

Surprised when he found it, on the table next to the window was a pot of still simmering stew along with a loaf of bread and a glass of water. Strange he was sure that table had been empty when he had first come into the room.

And even as tired as he had been he found it hard to believe that anyone could have come into the room without waking him. And if Buck had brought the food in without disturbing his sleep, it seemed even stranger that he would not have woke him to let him know? For that matter why would he have brought such a meal to his guest in the middle of the night?

Huh, all good questions that he would have to figure out later, as his rumbling stomach reminded him that it had been days since he had last eaten. A bowl and spoon sat next to the pot of stew, Ashes wasted no time in helping himself to a large portion of the stew. Ripping the loaf of bread in half he sat back on the bed and hungrily wolfed down the meal in quick bites.

When he had finished he stared at the empty bowl both surprised and embarrassed he had not realized just how hungry he had been. Sheepishly he looked back over at the pot on the table, even though he was no longer hungry it seemed wasteful to let the rest of the stew go uneaten. Limping back to the stew he started to fill his bowl a second time then stopped in mid scoop looking hard at the stew swimming in the pot.

At first, he was not sure but a closer look and deep sniff confirmed his suspicions. Jubilee stew! His mother had made this same stew when they were children. The last time he had eaten it was when he was ten years old just before she died. In all his life he had never found it anywhere else.

"Sometimes the memories from our childhood are the most cherished are they not?" Ashes turned on heel to face the speaker, forgetting for the second time that day about his injuries. His leg gave way under him sending stumbling sideways strong arms caught him steadying him.

Getting his balance he snapped at their owner "Not that I don't appreciate the help, or the meal, but you could knock or warn a person somehow instead of just sneaking up on them I have seen men get killed doing that!"

Glaring up he stopped in mid-sentence the smiling face looking back at him was not the one he had expected.

"My apologies friend it was not my intention to startle you." The newcomer said "It has been a long time since I have walked these halls and I am afraid my manners are rusty. But I don't think I need to worry about dying anymore," Stepping back he dipped his head respectfully in Ashes direction. "I am honored to meet you King Ashes I am Domino, Bucks younger brother."

The man standing in front of him resembled Buck a great deal it was easy to believe that they were brothers but hadn't Buck said that besides the horses and Desert cats he lived alone here? And even more concerning this man just called him "King Ashes" how could anyone alive know about that?

First things first he decided "Your Bucks younger brother?" He ask "Buck never said anything about anyone else living here." Ashes paused" And why did you call me a king? I am an ex-mercenary nothing more."

Domino chuckled softly "To answer your first question that is because I have not lived here in over fifteen hundred years." Reaching over he picked up the cup of water and offered it to Ashes. "And as for your second question, there are few who walk in the place that I walk now who does not know of Zalora and its great king. I know you have a lot of questions and there is much you need to know, for you will play a very important part in what must be done, but for now please believe me when I say that we have very little time."

Taking the offered water Ashes sat back on the bed. "That is the second time someone has said something like that in as many days, what is happening, and how do I have anything to do with it?"

Domino walked over to look out the window speaking over his shoulder "Stormracer told you of what this land once was and it can be again. Buck has the power to break the curse even if he does not realize it. But to do so he will need your help, yours and others, who like you do not yet know the parts they will play. Molder who tricked my brother into releasing the curse on this land, like Buck still lives and rules the kingdom Hagbill. But he is not a true immortal, every ten years he must renew his pledge to the one who gives him endless life. He does that with the power he steals from another. You have heard of the great Frolla trial?"

Ashes considered before he answered "I don't know many men who have not heard of it, it is the most famous race in any of the known kingdoms and the most deadly. I have never seen it myself but I heard that most of the men who enter the torment are either crippled or killed. But the prize is said to be worth the risk."

Domino nodded at the empty bowl sitting on the bed next to Ashes "Do you wish more?' Shaking his head Ashes handed the empty bowl to him.

Sitting it on the table, Domino muttered, "No amount of wealth is worth a life. But what Molder offers is a treasure beyond measure. More than any man knows, Or could comprehend, a horse sculpted from a pure diamond."

"Never gave it much thought, to be honest just passed it off as a wild tale like most such stories you hear of. Or I used to anyway, after the last few weeks." Ashes shrugged. "I always thought that it was one of the more foolhardy ones.

There is no way I know of to sculpt diamond, cut it yes, polish it, but not sculpt it. Though I heard stories that say it was not made by mortal hands. Something about lighting striking a mountain in the middle of a battle, between Molder's armies and some invaders.

The story says that the lighting spared Molder and his men but killed all of their enemies. That there was nothing left of them when the dust settled, just a great hole in the ground with the statue of a horse made from solid diamond sitting the bottom."

"There are many tales and many truths." Domino told him. "This one is a little of both, The statue that Molder offers is indeed crafted by God's will, but It was not God's touch that turned her to diamond it was my brothers."

Ashes consider thoughtfully "Bucks? I have never seen a mage with my own eyes, but even so, he does not strike me as one, especially one who would do such a thing."

Picking up the cup of water Domino offered it to Ashes "And you still have not, my brother is not a mage. My brother has walked this life a very long time but he is just a man both now and long ago when he listened to one he trusted and brought Stormracer down from the sky."

After taking a long drink from the cup Ashes sit it on the floor by the bed, "You're telling me that the diamond statue that Molder is offering as a prize is Stormracer? Or was her I mean."

Stepping towards Ashes Domino Spoke softly.

"There is much you need to know, much that cannot be explained with words. If you will allow it I can show you everything you must know I can let you see through my eyes my memories. All that happened."

Ashes hesitated. "I am not sure what you mean, a vision?"

Domino placed his hand on Ashes shoulder "That and much more, what I lived you will live. It will seem like years but in reality be but moments, will you allow it?" Ashes nodded hesitantly "You do not have to do this." Domino told him. "If you wish you can leave this place as soon as you are well enough, and no one will think any worse of you. The choice is yours."

"No!" Ashes replied "I admit that I don't understand all that is happening here just yet. But I do know that whatever it is, somehow it affects more than just this place, even if I overlooked the fact I owe Buck and Stormracer my life. And if I left, at some point I would have to face this threat."

Domino nodded, "Unfortunately you are right the one Molder serves grows in power he nurtures the wars and hate that is growing in this world, and feeds off the death and suffering they bring. This dessert is proof of that. Every day with every death it grows only a few feet a day, but even a few feet add up to miles over the years and with it as well grows his power. And he, in turn, rewards those who serve him with protection, wealth and power. As long as they are useful to him, but when their usefulness runs out. He takes back that that he gave them. And devours them body and soul. Molder is one of his most loyal servants and has been for a millennia. He believes that he is above such a fate, he is wrong as he will one day find out with your help. In a fortnight the tournament starts when it is over Molder will be stronger than ever. But right now he is weakened."

"What I don't understand is if Molder is growing stronger every tournament why have you waited till now to stop him?" Ashes ask. "Wouldn't it have been easier to stop him when this first started? Why wait till now when he is even more powerful?'

Domino smiled grimly, "Till now not all the pieces were in place, this tournament is a very important one for Molder. His master demands a far bigger price this time for his favors. And Buck needed to understand his part, you and China both are needed for your parts as well which you will learn soon. And those who are to help you also needed to be ready, even if they do not know yet the part they are to play."

"Others?" Ashes ask.

Domino nodded "Friends and allies that you have met before." Domino chuckled. "Though they have yet to meet you."

Ashes grinned ruefully. "At one time I would have thought a man a fool to say such a thing. Very well, I will do what you ask, to be honest, I am kind of curious to see what this place used to look like. If it even comes close to the stories it would be a wonder to behold."

Domino sat his hands on Ashes shoulders. "It was that and much more. But remember what you will see, you will see through my eyes, my memories. You will be but an observer, close your eyes sleep. When you wake you will know all that has happened in this land and what must be done to return it to what it once was."

Ashes felt himself falling into a deep sleep, like none he felt before, he was drifting in a warm darkness that seemed to pull him from his body. Just as the last slip of consciousness left him he heard Domino's voice in his head.

"The past cannot be changed only learned from, learn now my friend understand."

Chapter Five
The Legend of StormRacer

A rapid knock woke Domino from a deep sleep, confused he sat up in his bed rubbing his eyes. The sun was not even up yet why would anyone be waking him at this hour? "Wh- Whose there?" he muttered sleepy. "Go away! It is not even morning yet."

The door flung open revealing two figures outlined by the light from the lamp that the larger of the two was holding. The smaller of the two, Buck his older brother, by three years ran over to his bed pulling the blankets off him. "Come on Sugar britches get a move on! If you make us miss seeing her I will pound you good!"

Domino sat up suddenly. "You and who else butt face if you remember I beat you in our last fight!"

Putting his hands against his younger brother's chest Buck shoved him back against the mattress. "Only because I slipped sugar britches and I felt sorry for you because I beat you all the time!"

His mother Queen Shay, followed Buck into the room holding the lamp in front of her. The flickering flame lighting up the room "Alright!" she told the older brother "What have I told you about calling you brother that? And no one is going to pound anyone, got it? And you Domino... Butt-face? Really? Where did you pick that up? Never mind don't tell me, I think I already know. I swear if your father were still alive there are times I would slap him for teaching you two such things!" Looking around the room she found her sons pants and boots on the floor lying on top of a pile of clothes and handed them to him. "And both of your rooms are a filthy mess. Anyone who didn't know better would think that it was two-year-olds living in them not a nine and twelve-year-old boys, after the morning meal you two are both going to clean your rooms before you do anything else!"

As Domino hurriedly slipped into his pants and boots Buck muttered mutinously "I thought that was the servant's job. I mean what is the point of having servants if we have to clean our own rooms?"

Shay who had started to gather up some of the scattered clothing lying around the room suddenly stopped glaring at the older of the two brothers. "What did you just say? Do you want to apologize to the servants yourself for that, or do you want me to do it for you? Seeing as how if don't change your attitude right now you will be spending the rest of your VERY, SHORT, LIFE, in your room! Starting right now, and you will NOT get the chance to see her like this again till you are twenty, If I am not still mad at you then!"

Buck dropped his eyes avoiding his mother's glare. "I'm sorry, mother, I was excited and got carried away, please don't make me miss this."

The anger faded from Shays eyes sighing she placed a gentle hand on each of her sons heads "I understand being excited I am too, but you can't let being excited or angry cloud your mind when you speak, this time it was a simple comment no one was hurt but one day Buck you will be king, and a simple slip of judgment in a moment of anger could cost lives. I know you both are still young but I am counting on you both to help each other when you grow up. I won't always be here for you, you are going to have to be there for each other promise me that. Okay?"

Buck and Domino exchanged a begrudging look "I promise." Buck said

"Yea, I promise to" Domino muttered.

"Good," Shay smiled reaching down she took Domino's hand in hers leading the way out the door. "Now come on we need to hurry, it is almost morning. She will be here any minute."

Shay hurried through the castle halls with her sons in tow finally stepping out onto a balcony overlooking a large courtyard. Domino could hear the excitement in the voices of the people who filled it from wall to wall. Many like Shay were holding lamps casting an eerie glow on the faces both young and old all staring expertly towards the soft glow of the eastern sky heralding the coming morning. Then almost on cue, the courtyard fell silent the only sound coming from the tinkling of the fountain in the garden in the center of the courtyard.

As thousands of eyes watched the glow started moving across the sky slowly at first but growing faster with every second like a wave on the beach, pushing back the darkness of the night and lighting up the sky with the first light of the morning sun. Domino stared hard at the morning sky searching like everyone else, trying to catch a glimpse of the reason they were here.

Like a slow-moving ocean wave, the first light of morning rolled crossed the sky. The night darkness giving way before it. Queen Shay stood between her sons on the balcony. A hand on each son's shoulder Domino could feel her hand trembling with excitement as she searched the eastern sky with anxious eyes. For what seemed like an eternity the sky remained empty Buck looked up at his mother "Are you sure that she is coming? Maybe this is the wrong day."

Stroking her son's hair Shay whispered, "Have faith son she will be here. Remember hers is no ordinary journey."

"I know." Buck whispered, "Everyone says she lives in the heavens that she is one of God's own horses. What if God says she can't visit us this time? He wouldn't do that would he?"

Leaning down Shay gave her son a gentle kiss on the cheek. "No, he would not. Not without reason. Be patient just a little longer and have faith she will be here I promise."

The words were barely out of her mouth. When the guard on the watchtower shouted pointing excitedly. "There! There she is!" Domino stared hard trying desperately to see what the guard was seeing. Even though the sun had not risen completely the morning light was almost blinding.

Laughing Shay put a hand In front of both of her son's eyes shading them. "Don't stare at the sun both of you, do you want to go blind?" Nodding with her head. "Over there, see? To the right of the Sun just over the foothills. There she is, she is coming this way!"

Following his mother's gaze, Domino saw what till now he had only heard of in stories and tales, Stormracer! Running towards the castle Bucking and tossing her head in joy playing in the light of the rising sun running not on the ground but in the air. Domino light headed with excitement barely heard his brother only a few feet away "She came, she really came!" Rushing to the edge of the balcony he leaned over waving his arms over his head shouting, "Stormracer OVER HERE!"

Domino could feel the excitement in the air as Stormracer galloped towards the packed courtyard. Soft rolling thunder echoed with every beat of her hooves even though they never once struck the ground. Just as he thought she going to run right past them without stopping she veered their way each stride of her hooves bringing her that much closer to the ground. Carrying her over the heads of the people in the courtyard below before finally settling down on the balcony next to the queen and her sons.

The big balcony suddenly seemed much smaller as the mare settled gracefully down Shay and her sons stepped back to make room for her imposing bulk. Dominos breath caught in his throat there were dozens of murals and paintings of the great mare in the palace but none even came close to capturing her true beauty. Stormracer was not an overly big mare standing about sixteen hands at the shoulder pert small ears sat on a finely chiseled head with both a long flowing tail and mane.

That is where her resemblance to mortal horse ended her coat was an ever-swirling mix of silver and white in constant motion as if the very clouds were moving through her body. Her main and tail blew away from her body even when she was standing still. Caught up in an unseen wind.

But it was her eyes that held Dominos attention a beautiful deep mix of blue and green with gold pupils light up by never-ending sparks of light deep within them. As if all the lightning storms in the world were held inside those glowing orbs that seemed to memorize anyone who looked into them

Domino jerked in surprise as a voice both deep and breezy filled his head. "Hail queen Shay, Hail prince Buck and young prince Domino." Turning her head to look out over the courtyard she let out a joyful whinny. "And hail to the good people of Brutus-hay I am honored to walk among you again!"

The courtyard was filled with the deafening roar of thousands of voices cheering and yelling greetings in return. Stepping forward with a graceful curtsy Shay smiled, "Forgive the noise good mare they are happy to see you, as am I, it has been too long since we were blessed with your presence."

"There is nothing to forgive" Came the reply. "I only wish that the time I walked among you was not so brief." Domino felt his stomach tighten as the mare turned her gaze on Buck and him. "Your sons are growing up to be strong young men good queen, soon they will be as fine a man as your husband Dragon was."

"There are times I wonder my lady" Shay told her glancing at her two sons. "But they are learning though, I do very much miss Dragon." Hesitantly she added, "Does he walk the same lands you do, does he ever speak of this world?"

"He does indeed walk in Gods lands daughter and he sends his love," Stormracer told her sympathetically" In time you will be reunited with him, but not just yet. You are needed here your sons need your patience and guidance and your people need your wisdom."

"Thank you, both for your kind words and for bringing me Dragons message." Shay told her smiling" And not to worry I have no intention of passing on to the next world just yet, for one thing, I don't want to have to answer to God for setting these two loose on the kingdom just yet."

Domino did not know whether to feel proud of the complement Stormracer had given them or embarrassed by his mother's words. He had always been very proud of his father even though he had not got the chance to truly know him.

Dragon died when a band of raiders had attacked an outlying town killing most of the men and taking the women prisoners. Attacks on Brutus-hay were very rare most of the other kingdoms were peaceful with them.

Brutis-hay was a very wealthy land with a very powerful army, but it was not fear of its army that kept the peace. It was mostly because of Stormracer that the land was blessed with more food than they could eat a blessing they shared with the surrounding kingdoms asking nothing in return. An arrangement that none of the great kingdom's neighbors wanted to risk in a foolish attack. That could not be said for the bands of roving thieves that heard of the wealth and generosity of the land. Lusting after the first and foolishly believing the second to be a sign of weakness.

His father took one hundred men and went after them catching up to them on the first day. The fight was short, Dragon's men quickly overwhelming the thieves and freeing the women, all but one. The last of the thieves managed to break away from the fighting and grab up a young girl as he fled on his horse. Dragon saw what was happening and gave chase with several of his men following what they did not know was the thieves had a man scouting the trail ahead. Hearing the fighting and not wanting to risk his own life in a hopeless battle. He had hidden himself in a grove to wait to see what the outcome of the battle would be.

Seeing which way the battle was going he decided to wait till it was over and salvage whatever he could from his fallen companions after the King and his men had left. When he saw the last of the thieves fleeing and the King gave chase, it was a chance he could not pass up. It was said there was a reward of one thousand gold coins to the man who killed Brutus-hays King. Normally he would not have taken the risk but the king was well ahead of his men and it was an easy shot.

Dragon caught up to the fleeing thief and with a quick throw of his dagger, he brought the chase to an end, hitting the man in the back of his neck and knocking him off his horse. As he fell he pulled the young girl off the galloping horse with him both of them hitting the ground. The thief was dead before he hit the ground, he was beyond feeling any pain from the fall. Dragons concern was for the young girl who when she tried to stand up after the fall stopped grabbing her leg with a painful gasp and started to stagger sideways, the bone just above her ankle thrusting through the side of her young leg.

Swinging off his horse Dragon ran to her catching her before she fell then gently laid her on the ground to inspect her leg with his back to the last of the thieves hidden in the trees. His men were only twenty feet away when they spotted the man and yelled a warning. The warning came too late, the king spun around just as the thief loosed his arrow he could have jumped away from the arrows path but if he did the arrow would surely hit the young girl who could not get out of its way. Dragon had the choice of stepping aside to save his own life or to stand his ground using his own body to shield the girl, to him it was an easy choice.

Dragon was a brave man who cared for his people he stood his ground the arrow burying itself deep in his chest. The kingdom mourned their King's loss and the tales of his sacrifice traveled far that day.

As queen, the duty of caring for the kingdom and its people fell on Shay a task that she did not ask for but accepted, and did well. Domino suspected though that on Bucks twentieth birthday she would be relieved to hand that responsibility over to the young

Prince.

Stormracer blew out gently startling Domino and bringing him out of his thoughts. "Wake up Sugar britches." Buck laughed.

"Sorry" Domino stuttered looking embarrassingly at the mare. "I was thinking of father."

Stormracer's gentle voice filled his head. "Don't apologize I understand child. I said it is hard to believe as big as you are that it is only your tenth birthday you will be celebrating. "A rush of pride filled him both by the compliment and the fact that Stormracer had known.

Shay smiled proudly, "They are both growing fast good mare, almost too fast they are sometimes more than a handful."

Stormracer's laughing nicker filled the air. "All young are daughter, but cherish the young for it is in teaching them that we learn. Now walk with me, I have a whole kingdoms people to visit and but a day to do so."

Buck fell in beside his brother as they followed. "Are you alright? I thought you fell asleep just now."

Domino gave his brother a gentle shove. "I'm fine like I said I was just thinking about father sometimes I really miss him."

Buck put a comforting hand on his younger brothers shoulder, "Yea me too. But mom needs us to be strong were not kids anymore."

Feeling uncomfortable Domino changed the subject, "She's really beautiful isn't she?"

Bucks breath seemed to catch in his throat.

"Very!" he replied passionately "I have never seen anything more beautiful could you imagine what it would be like to ride such a Horse?"

Domino was truly shocked. "Ride her?" he stuttered. "Buck how can you even think that? No one can ride her! It is forbidden to even touch her! Mother told both of us that."

Buck shrugged. "I know but you and I both heard the stories about in the past people have ridden her the great King Orie was said to have ridden her the day he died."

Domino elbowed his older brother in the ribs. "The story said that she carried him to heaven dummy she can do that sometimes, he was already dead. Man, you really are dumb some days."

"Not as dumb as you!" Buck reported elbowing his younger brother back. Domino opened his mouth reply when he saw Shay glaring at them over her shoulder there was no mistaking the promise in that look if they continued with their argument. Both boys fell silent stepping away from each other.

The people on either side of the bottom of the stairs stepped aside their heads dipping in respect as they passed. Stormracer truly enjoyed being among the people stopping every so often to talk to one or the other. Domino could not help but notice that no matter who it was she would stop to talk to she greeted as a close friend and seemed to know a great deal about their lives and would listen to their concerns.

"She really does care about us doesn't she?" Domino asked his mother

"She loves us." Shay answered him, "And the people love her God blessed us with her, and is trusting us to protect her as she protects us." Turning to face her sons Shay put a hand softly on their shoulders giving a quick glance back at Stormracer who was deep in conversation with several people, "I need both of you to promise me here and now that you will protect her make sure that no one ever tries to hold or touch her ." She told them fervently, "She is far more than just a horse she is pure and innocent and there are those who would do anything to own her. That cannot happen! Buck, you above all must promise me, soon you will be king and there are those who will try to lure you and trick you into believing nothing will happen if you try to hold her. That is not true! This land is blessed in its bounty only because of her and it is said that if ANYONE tries to hold her this land will burn. Many a king and queen have thought of what it would be like to ride such an animal but they put aside that temptation, you must also! Please not only for this kingdoms sake but for her own, promise me now you will keep her safe!"

Both Buck and Domino were surprised by the intensity in their mother's voice and the pleading in her eyes, in all their young lives they had never before seen her this way. "

"I promise!" Buck told her

"So do I," Domino said

Looking both embarrassed and relived Shay leaned close and gave both of her sons a quick kiss on the cheek before either one could step away. "Mother!" Buck said wiping his forearm across his face.

"Do you have to do that where everyone can see?"

Smiling Shay turned to catch up to Stormracer who was surrounded by a large group of troubled looking people. Making her way through them Shay could see why a young girl was standing in front of the mare crying as she held up the limp form of a puppy that could not be more than a few months old. "Please, Miss Stormracer Please, he is the last one left of his litter all the others died, the healers could not do anything for them." She sobbed. "And they say that there is nothing they can do for him. Father said it would be wrong to ask you to help him if it is I'm sorry, but please he is only a puppy and I love him can't you do anything?"

Stormracer lowered her head toward the girl. "Child there is no wrong in wanting to save another's life, or in asking for help in doing so. I will do what I can but you must understand that if it is God's will there is nothing I will be able to do, I can but try."

Hugging the puppy the girl nodded "I understand." She whispered. "I will miss him but I understand."

"Good." Stormracer told her. "You're a brave girl." looking around she nodded towards a bench sitting along the near wall. "Sit him down on that bench." Doing as she was told the girl sit the puppy gently down and stepped back away from it. The pups head rolled to one side the only sign of life was a weak whimper. Stepping forward Stormracer lowered her head staring intently at the pup, Domino held his breath as the air around the pup began to shimmer, and a sudden breeze blew the leaves off the nearby trees pulling them with it to form a small fast moving spiral that danced above the puppy's still form.

Then as suddenly as it had come the breeze was gone the dancing leaves falling to form a green blanket covering the puppies still form. Lifting her head Stormracer silently stepped back away from the pup Domino could not tell from looking at her if she had been successful, did the pup die after all? Just as he was starting to think it had, the leaves stirred as the pup lifted its head with a questioning yap.

The girl ran forward throwing her arms around the pup. "Corkie! Oh, Corkie, you are ok!" Picking up the pup she turned to Stormracer. "He is going to be ok isn't he?"

"Yes." The mare told her. "The illness is gone, but he is going to be weak for a few days you are going to have to let him sleep and regain his strength."

"I will Stormracer, thank you!" Turning she broke into a run carrying the puppy before stopping to face the mare again "Sorry, I almost forgot." She said apologetically barely avoiding tripping as she gave a clumsy cruise while trying to hold onto the pup.

"Thank you good mare" Shay told her. "That was a great kindness and one she will not likely forget."

Stormracer nickered. "I did nothing but take the illness from the pups body God is the one that chose to let him remain with the child, I cannot and will not go against his will."

The rest of the day passed quickly without incident. When the day ended the people of kingdom gathered to see her off sad to see her leaving but understanding why, "Farewell good mare. "Shay told her," Till the day when you can visit us once more.'

Leaping off the balcony Stormracer's hooves caught the air as surely as if they had struck the ground carrying her above the crowd, "A great day that will be for your kingdom lady Shay". She replied turning her gaze on Buck, "For on that day also you will welcoming a new king!" The courtyard was once again filled with the yells of farewell from the people below as with ever-increasing strides she disappeared into the setting sun.

"That was a good block prince but you were slow in recovering your balance an enemy could easily catch you off guard if you are not quicker" Domino straightened up getting his feet firmly back under him to face the speaker bringing his sword back at the ready position.

It had been five years since Stormracer had visited the kingdom and he has spent the last three both training in combat and studying in the laws and diplomacy of the kingdom. He would be turning fourteen in just a few weeks and even though it was Buck who was to soon be king, Queen Shay insisted that he learn the nuances of the kingdom as well. Combat training was his favorite he enjoyed the challenge.

Lancer was both his teacher and instructor a slender middle age man who at one time been a very good thief. His luck run out when he tried to sneak into the castle treasury and had misjudged how long it took for the guards to complete their rounds. Hearing the guards returning he tried to make his getaway he was caught halfway out the window with a very large bag of gold tied to his back.

The queen had sentenced him to five years for his crime, but changed her mind after talking to the man. His easy manner and well spoke words gave her an idea, her sons needed a tutor. And this man though admittedly a thief, struck her as a good candidate so she gave him his choice. Take her stubborn sons under wing and educate them or spend the next five years in prison.

With the understanding that if he tried in any way to take advantage of the situation his sentence would be fifty years. Lancer agreed and the boys got a tutor who was very patient and understanding when his student needed extra help with his lessons Domino liked the man.

Lancer raised his own sword bracing himself. "Alright, young Prince comes at me again this time remember to brace your off foot when you block."

Just as Domino readied his charge a familiar voice interrupted them. "Excuse me, Lancer, can I speak to my son for a moment?" looking over his shoulder Domino saw his mother riding Bee-bop a two-tone stallion that Dragon had given her for her thirtieth birthday.

Straightening up Lancer dipped his head. "Of course my queen Domino we will pick up where we left off when you are ready."

Shay smiled at the man with a reply of "Thank you I will just be a moment." Glancing at Domino Shay ask, "Have you seen your brother this morning?" Her smile and easy tone did little to hide the annoyance in her eyes.

"Buck?" Domino ask innocently.

"Yes, Buck! Do you have any other brothers?" Shay snapped glaring at him.

Taken aback by her angry tone Domino muttered, "Sorry mother not since morning meal he said he had something to do and left on starlight, I think he was heading…"

"I know where he was heading. "Shay interrupted." The same place he goes every morning to see if he can spot her I was hoping he would get beyond this." She added with a sigh. "Lord Bane the Silverton king is going to be here shortly and Buck is supposed to greet them with me."

"Do you want me to find him?" Domino ask. "I think he is on the East Ridge I could find him and be back by midday."

Shay considered. "No, not alone, the scouts have reported sightings of bands of thieves in the area. They have been getting more and bolder since dragons death. I sent out several guardsmen this morning to deal with them but best not to take chances "Looking back at her escort she nodded, "We will go with you no band of thieves no matter how many will chance a fight with the royal escort." Domino had to agree the men given the honor of guarding his mother were among the best and deadliest in the royal services.

Sheathing his sword he gathered up Nipper a pretty black mare with more attitude than many stallions. Swinging up into the saddle he watched as Lancer tried vainly to catch Carter a gray and white stallion a big strong horse but with a very Independent streak. Domino wondered if the man did not spend more time chasing the stud than he did riding him, after a five-minute chase involving Lancer and half the Royal escort they cornered the horse and were on their way.

"Ok." Shay said. "If we are ready let's go get your brother. "Pulling her horse head around she headed east.

Domino hesitated before saying, "If you are heading for the east ridge I don't think we will find him there."

Reigning her horse in Shay looked back at her son. "He watching for her on the East Ridge is he not?"

Domino hesitated, "No, not right now I don't think."

Shay looked confused. "You don't think? I thought he went to the East Ridge first thing every morning to watch for her if that is not where he is, where is he and what is he doing?"

"Oh, he does wait on the east ridge in the morning but not all morning," Domino said quickly.

"Domino!" Shay said exasperatedly. "I am starting to lose my patience you had better start making sense, where is he?"

Suddenly uncomfortable Domino lowered his gaze. "Uhh, proudly Boga lake that is where he meets Shilo."

"Shilo?" Shay said confused. "And who may I ask is Shilo?"

"Uhh." Domino hesitated before continuing. "I kind of promised not to tell anyone." he said miserably.

Shay nudged Bee-bop with her foot and the stallion bounded forwarded until she was within reach of her son. Reaching over she put a hand under his chin and gently but firmly lifted his head to look him in the eye.

"It is a little too late to worry about broken promises right now isn't it? What you need to worry about is me, because if you do not start explaining right now you are going to be VERY sorry! Do you understand me, young man?"

 Swallowing nervously Domino nodded "Shilo is a girl he met about four moons ago, he really likes her she is pretty and really nice, they meet every morning and almost every day. He didn't want me to tell you because he did not know how you would react to him being with the armors daughter." He explained in a rush.

"I see." Shay said tightly. "And the two of you thought it would be a good idea to keep secrets from me and lie to me rather than tell me the truth is that it?"

Unable to meet his mother's angry stare Domino dropped his eyes, "We were going to tell you Buck just wanted to wait a while he really likes Shilo and doesn't want to have to stop seeing her."

The anger slowly faded from Shays eyes as she dropped her hand from her son's chin. "I guess this is partly my fault." She said thoughtfully. "Well no use getting angry about it now I suppose, him being with this young women is in a small way better than him sitting all morning on a ridge watching for Stormracer. Very well let's go meet this girl and introduce ourselves shall we?" Tugging on the reins she pulled Bee-bops head around and headed off in the direction of Boga Lake at a canter.

Boga Lake was a large lake fed by three different rivers, the only outlet being a large glory hole in the center.

It was said that the waters entering that fast-moving whirlpool emptied out at Thunder falls fifty miles from the lake. No one knew for sure and no one was willing to risk their lives to find out. The lake itself was a beautiful sight sitting at the bottom of a large canyon and surrounded by forest on all sides.

It was in the first morning and evening light that it was the most impressive though, with the sun's rays shining on the spinning waters the glory hole made a breathtaking sight to anyone looking at it. But it was not the glory hole that their party came looking for.

With Shay leading the way the group made their way along the lake bank looking for Buck and Shilo, it was Shay who first spotted them as they crested a large hill.

Domino riding aside and slightly behind his mother was the first to see the look on her face when she topped the ridge, a look of surprise and shock followed by anger, following her gaze he saw the reason why. Standing facing them waist deep in water was Buck and

Shilo both looking surprised and scared and both completely naked.

The rest of the search party reined in behind Shay all with the same shocked looks on their faces, "Mother!" Buck stuttered. "We…we…were just…we didn't…we never..."

Glaring Shay threw a hand up, "STOP!" she snapped. "Just stop, I don't care what you have to say, I don't want to hear it! The best thing both of you can do right now is just keep quiet". Shilo had sunk down in the water up to her neck till only her head was exposed, "A little late for vanity is it not young lady?" Shay growled. Looking like she wished the glory hole had swallowed her Shilo nodded.

Turning her attention back to her son Shay spoke with an eerie calm All the more frighten for it. "Now what you to are going to do is get dressed get on your horses and take your disobedient selves back to the castle, where we will discuss this there and if you both are lucky I might be in a calmer mood by then, but don't count on it!" Looking both scared and embarrassed Buck waded out of the lake Shilo stayed where she was looking unsure, "Did you not hear me, young lady?" Shay snapped.

"Yes, my queen," Shilo muttered. Shyly she nodded at the watching guards.

Shay glared back at the man. "Shouldn't you be watching for thieves?" She half shouted. "Turn your heads!"

With the guards looking the other way Shilo waded out of the water to stand next to Buck, both of them quickly started to get dressed ignoring the fact that they were still dripping wet. "Well," Domino offered. "At least you can't say she is trying to hide anything from us"

Shay whipped her head around to fix her son with a piercing glare, "Don't think that you are not in trouble ether young man, You may find this amusing Domino but I do not, I will be talking to you about keeping secrets from me right after I deal with your brother." Sighing Domino backed Nipper away from his seething mother.

The ride back to the castle was a long silent one no one wanting to risk making the queen any angrier than she already was. Riding beside his mother Domino could see her looking back at Buck and Shilo from time to time riding at the rear of the column. The anger in her eyes replaced by a thoughtful pondering look.

They were less than a mile from the castle when a small group of riders met them. "'My queen."

Skyblue, the captain of the city guard riding in the lead greeted them, "Lord Bane arrived just a short while ago I told him that you had been unavoidably delayed and apologized. He seemed to understand but he is waiting in the main hall. I told the servants to see to their needs while we tried to find you. I hope that is alright."

Nodding Shay told the man, "You did well Skyblue." She said looking at the setting sun. "Will you please ride ahead and inform him that I will not be able to meet with him tonight." Glaring back at Buck and Shilo. "Tell him with my apologies that I have pressing family matters I need to see to and I will gladly speak with him at first light, if it can be arranged, and see to it that he and his party needs are met."

Dipping his head Skyblue nodded at her, "It will be as you say my lady." Pulling his horses head around he headed back for the castle at a gallop to deliver the message.

Sighing Shay called back over her shoulder, "Romeo!" Waiting as the young guard brought his horse alongside her before she went on, "Ride ahead and find the armorer Thunk till him I want to see him in the throne room as soon as he can get there."

Looking back at Shilo Romeo nodded, "As you wish my lady, may I say something?"

"Go ahead," Shay said absently

Hesitantly Romeo went on, "My queen I know Thunk he is a good man, I don't think that he knew of this."

Smiling Shay put a hand on Romeo's arm, "You are worried that I mean to punish the father for the daughter's mistake?" She chuckled, "I have no intention of doing so, but I do think that he should be part of any decision that is made about this, don't you?" Looking relieved Romeo nodded. "Good," Shay said, "Now please give him the message."

After watching Romeo ride off Shay trotted Be-bop the rest of the way back to the castle deep in thought when they reached the stables she slid off the stallion absently handing the reins to a surprised groom. Since the king's death Shay had always insisted on handling the stallion herself for her to let anyone else work with him was unheard of. Thanking the man she headed off toward the castle only stopping long enough to look back at Domino. "Make sure your brother and Shilo remember that I want to see them as soon as they get their horses taken care of."

"You mean to see more of them than you did at the lake?" He ask under his breath. Domino felt a moment of panic as Shay stopped mid-step and half turned to face him. Had she heard him?

Glaring at her son Shay muttered "When I see your father again...." Without another word she headed off in the direction of the throne room.

After Passing on the message to Shilo and Buck the three made sure to get every hair brushed on their mounts trying to convince themselves that it was not because they were nervous about facing the queen. Still, there was only so much brushing that could be done on a horse and after delaying as long as possible they made their way to the throne room.

Shay was waiting for them when they got to the throne room standing in front of a picture of a younger Dragon and herself on the rear wall, not sitting on the great throne at the end of the room like Domino had expected... "Well, those must be some very clean horses." Shay commented "Buck will you please close the doors?" Glancing at Domino, Buck undid the heavy decorative chains holding the doors open and pulled them shut. The room echoed with the sound of the soft thud as they closed. "Good," Shay said, "I don't think that there is any need for anyone else to be involved in this do you, good Thunk?"

All three of them jumped when a voice answered from behind them and Thunk stepped out of the shadows, "No my queen this is a personal matter between us and our children no one else."

"Well then," Shay said, "Let's get on with this then shall we?" Without waiting for an answer she went on. Fixing Buck and Shilo with a hard look she asked "How Far has this gone?"

Looking uncertain Buck and Shilo glanced at each other "How far?" Buck ask innocently "What do you mean?"

Stepping forward Shay said softly "I am trying very hard to be fair about this Buck it would be wise for you not to act the fool, but if you want me to be clear very well." Giving both of them a hard stare she went on, "Have the two of you bedded together?

"What!" Buck yelped

"No, my queen we have not!" Shilo said obviously embarrassed.

"At least not yet." Shay said knowingly. "Tell me both of you what would have happened if we had not found you when we did?

Could you have still denied it after today?"

"Yes, we could have!" Buck said angrily "We were swimming in the lake, nothing more, just like we have done a lot of times in the past..." Suddenly looking sick Buck trailed off.

"We love each other but we really have not done anything like that my lady" Shilo said barely above a whisper, "At least not yet."

"Huh," Shay muttered studying the young couple "Very well; I believe you." It was hard for Domino to tell if Buck and Shilo looked more shocked or relieved. "I believe you," the queen repeated, "But that does not mean I approve of your actions, you both have been acting like foolish children! You say you have done this before and I have no trouble believing that as well. Did either one of you even bother to think of what would happen if it had been one of the bands of outlaws that are roaming the lands that had found you, and not us?" Not waiting for an answer she went on, "No, of course, you did not It never even crossed your minds did it?" Turning her head she fixed Buck with an angry stare, "You, my son would more than likely be killed on sight. I doubt that a band of thieves would know what the prince looked like to ransom him. After all, no one would expect a prince to be frolicking naked in a lake with a young woman unguarded, at least not an intelligent one." Turning her gaze to Shilo she muttered: "And you young lady after they had finished with you themselves they would more than likely have sold you to the slave markets in Libcorna were you would have spent the rest of your life wishing that they had killed you."

Buck and Shilo dropped their eyes looking cowered. With a deep sigh, Shay softened her voice, "I am not trying to be cruel. I am just trying to make you see the foolishness of your actions." Crossing the room she put a hand on each of their shoulders, "I have no desire to lose my son, and I am sure that Thunk would like to have his daughter around a bit longer." Dropping her hands she stepped back to look at Thunk who had moved to stand behind the two. "We are in agreement on what we discussed before, good Thunk?"

"Yes my queen," Thunk answered without hesitation.

"Good" Shay said turning around she walked to the smaller of the great thrones that dominated the room. Sitting in it she raised her voice to be heard clearly "I want both of you to listen very carefully to what I am going to say, don't talk listen. We have discussed this and here is what we have decided. The two of you may continue to see each other, if that is what you want, under these conditions. "Holding out her hand Shay counted off on her fingers. "One, you will remain clothed, Two when you go out together it will be with an escort, not because we don't trust you but to keep you safe, Three, you will not go out until you have finished you duties for the day, Buck that means all you studies, as well as any given task, and finally Four, you must promise, both of you, that if you feel you cannot keep your wants for each other under control you tell either myself or Thunk. We will figure out then what to do and you will not be punished for it." Lowering her hand Shay ask, "Do you think that you can do these things?"

"Yes mother," A surprised looking Buck said.

"Me as well my queen." Shilo added looking equally as surprised.

"Oh don't look so shocked." A half amused Shay said, "Both myself and Thunk we're young too once and we do understand, but it is time for both of you to stop acting like children and start being adults." Suddenly looking tired Shay waved a hand dismissively. "Now if you don't mind I have other problems to sort out yet."

As they were leaving the room Domino felt the hair on the back of his neck raise looking around he spotted Molder standing in the shadows of the throne room doors. Watching them leave. Molder was a thin grey-haired man but no one knew for sure how old he truly was. Everyone said that he had been one of his father's best friends and trusted adviser growing up. A kind generous man that everyone liked. But after Dragons death, he changed. No One knew why for sure but the man who he used to be was gone. Replaced by a cruel and untrustworthy man. Queen Shay tolerated him because he has been Dragons friend. But it was clear to anyone who saw them together that this was the only reason she let him remain in the castle service. Domino did not like or trust the man looking back over his shoulder he saw Molder heading into the throne room.

Dropping behind the others Domino waited until they turned the hall corner before ducking into a side passage that leads back to the throne room. The passage door let out just inside the throne room doors. Slipping inside he could hear his mother and Molder talking in strained tones he flattened himself against the wall to listen to what was being said.

"And I am telling you Molder it is not going to happen!" Shay snapped. "Brutus-hay has never made any of our neighbors pay for what we have in abundance and we are not going to start now!"

"In the past no we have not!" Molder shot back, "But time is changing the other kingdoms they don't share our sense of goodwill. What you see as a kindness they see as a weakness to take advantage of. Why do you think that there are bands of thieves roaming our lands now? They must be taught a lesson! Surely you see that!" Careful to stay hidden Domino inched closer watching Molder ready to defend his mother if necessary.

Shay still sat on the throne glaring at the man, "There is no proof that the bands of thieves in our lands are anything but just that roaming bands of scum with no ties to any of the other lands and I will not punish our friends for them!"

"Friends!" Molder laughed, "My lady they are anything but your friends. While you sit in your castle giving away the lands riches, I have been traveling the lands I have heard what they say. King Dragon they respected, but you they do not! And if you think they feel any kind of gratitude for your generosity then you are insanely blind! I came here today to try to reason with you not to argue if Dragon was still alive he would see the truth in what I am saying!"

Slamming her fist against the arms of the throne Shay sprang to her feet. "Do not tell me what my husband would think! I know what Dragon would have done and it would not be making the other lands pay ransom for the food they need to survive! God blessed us with Stormracer and she gives us an abundance of food and as long as I am queen we will not force anyone to pay for what God has given us! This discussion is over Molder and I warn you if you ever bring this up again you will find yourself exiled to the darkest dungeons for the rest of your life Dragons friend or not! Are we clear about that?"

Even from where he was standing Domino could feel the anger radiating from the man, "Yes my queen." Molder hissed, "Crystal clear." Without another word he spun around and stomped out of the room.

Shay watched glaring as Molder left the room before setting back down with an exhausted sigh. Looking at her from the shadows Domino realized he had never in all his life seen her looking vulnerable like this. His mother had always seemed so full of energy and life, never doubting herself even when Dragon had been killed. She had mourned but she did not let his death keep her from her duties as queen. Hesitantly he stepped out of the shadows. "Mother?"

Shays head jerked up surprised, "Domino" She said. "I thought you left with your brother how long have you been standing there?"

"Long enough," Domino told her. "I did leave with Buck but I saw Molder sneak in after we left I did not want to leave you alone with him."

A tired smile touched Shays' face. "My son." she muttered, "Do I really look so old that you think that I could not handle that fool? Remember I was not born a queen, I was born a guards daughter with no brothers, my father taught me how to defend myself VERY well." Holding out a hand she gestured at the empty seat next to her. "Come now, Sit with your old mother for a bit I could use someone to talk to about now."

Crossing over to sit next to his mother Domino hesitated looked uncertain at what once had been his father's throne. Since the day of his death, not even Shay had sit in it. "Go ahead," Shay said kindly understanding his reluctance. "I think your father would be proud to see you sitting there." Still, uncertain Domino lowered himself into the seat cushions.

Looking up at his mother he was surprised to see a distant sad look in her eyes. "Mother?" He said not able to keep the concern out of his voice.

Reaching over Shay patted him on the leg. "I am alright son I was just thinking how much you and Buck look like your father, sometimes I still expect to see him walk through those doors." She laughed. "Of course, if he was to, he would probably ask you what the hell you were doing sitting in his chair." Standing abruptly she reached over taking his hand in hers pulling him to his feet. "Come, It has been a long interesting day and I am tired and I am sure you are too, we both could use some sleep. Let's talk on the way to my room."

Getting to his feet he followed his mother out of the throne room. Looking back at him she waved her hand. "I said walk with me, not stalk me, Son get up here and walk next to your queen that is a royal command."

Catching up to her he ask hesitatingly "If you do not trust Molder why don't you simply tell him to leave or ban him from the castle?"

"Because he was you fathers closest friend. At one time they were like brothers I let him stay out of respect for your father," she added. "If I was to banish him from the castle it would be harder to keep track of his doings. With him close I can keep an eye on him and hopefully stop any trouble. Before he starts it."

"I guess I never thought of it that way." Domino told her. "But still, I don't think it is a good idea for you to be alone even in the castle. I saw the look in his eyes when he left the throne room just now, he hates you mother! I wouldn't put it past him to try to hurt you."

Putting her arm around her son Shay pulled him close. "My little protector." She smiled. "Don't worry, I don't think that Molder has the courage to try an attempt on my life. He knows what my sons would do to him if he succeeds and he knows what I would do to him if he failed." She laughed "So I think I am safe for now, it is your brother I am worried about. "Suddenly serious she stopped turning to Domino. "You are a thinker you think things through before you act. Buck is more like your father thinking more with his heart than his head. Most of the time there is no harm in that, but a king has to know the difference. Buck is a good young man and with your help, he will be a great king. But he likes Molder and listens to him that worries me.

The pleading look in his mother's eyes was almost overwhelming did she truly distrust Molder that much? "I won't always be around to keep an eye on Molder so I need you to do it for me. I want you to promise me, son, that you will watch out for your brother. Don't let Molder influence him because he will try, you need to be there Domino to stop that from happening. Promise me, son, that you will do that, please. When my time comes to pass into the next life I will do so easier if I know you are watching out for your brother."

"I promise mother." He told her softly, "I won't let Molder hurt him or anyone else not if I can do anything about it."

Sighing Shay leaned forward giving him a kiss on the forehead. "My little prince." she murmured. Slipping her arm around his she walked with him in silence the rest of the way down the long hallway. Till they reached her room putting her hand on the handle she turned to him. "I think I can make it safely the rest of the way." She told him smiling. "Thank you for the escort." Opening the door she stopped halfway in. "Oh, Domino, your duties for the next month are doubled." She told him chuckling. "Keeping secrets from your queen, remember?"

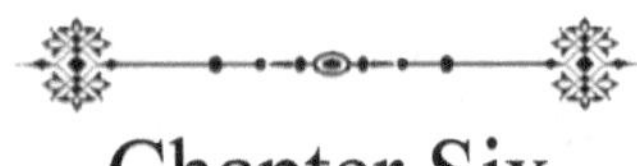

Chapter Six
The Rise of the a King, the fall of a Legend

Summers passed quickly without incident. Both Domino and Buck grew as did Bucks and Shilo's love for each other. Shilo a kind, gentle, woman had become VERY popular and well known with the people of the kingdom. So when it was announced that she and Buck would be wed on his coronation day the kingdom reacted with great enthusiasm.

The days leading up to the wedding was the busiest Domino had ever seen. It was hard to tell what the people were more excited about the coronation the wedding or Stormracer's return. Domino spent most of his waking hours trying to keep from being run over by the flood of servants and guest running through the castle hallways.

On the eve before the big day it was even more hectic than usual and for the fourth time in five minutes, Domino had to flatten himself against the wall to let a party pass. Grumbling he ducked into a side hall trying to get out of the way when he heard his mother calling him. "Domino have you seen Buck? I told him to meet me in his room a half hour ago and now I can't find him."

"He's probably stuck in the halls somewhere waiting to get by. I have not been able to get to my own room and I have been trying for a half day!" He growled.

Shay rolled her eyes sighing. "Really Domino, half a day? I saw you cross half the kingdom in that time to get out of greeting king Mulkies just last month, don't exaggerate."

"King Mulkies is the most annoying person alive," Domino said defensively. : "And you know it that is why you keep shoving him off on me."

"Remember who you are speaking to son," Shay said hauntingly. "I am your queen, beside I only ask you to meet with him so you can learn diplomacy, now stop complaining and see if you can find your brother."

Grumbling to himself Domino headed off in search of Buck after asking several people he finally found a chambermaid who had seen him. "The young king?" She ask. "Yes Lord Domino he said he wanted to be alone and was heading in the direction of the stables just a short while ago."

Thanking the girl Domino made his way thru the busy hallways to the stable. Searching through the large stable at first he thought that the chambermaid had told him wrong. Except for the horse's ether standing in their stalls or paddocks, the stables seemed empty. Just as he was turning to leave he heard voices coming from the back of the stable were the hay and grain was stored, the first voice he had no trouble recognizing Buck, and he knew the answering voice as well and had no love the owner, Molder.

Dominos first instinct was to leave and come back after Molder had left he had no desire to eavesdrop on his brother. Heading for the entrance he heard Molder's voice again. "It is a great honor my young king and a great responsibility your people will be lucky to have a king like you. Your mother is a good woman but she is stuck in the ways of the past and times have changed if Brutus-hay is to prosper it must change as well. I tried without success to explain this to Queen Shay but she would not hear it."

"Mother has always done what is best for the people Molder. I have no intention of doing otherwise the laws stand and I have no interest in changing them not without very good reason." Bucks' voice sounded uncertain and slightly annoyed.

"And. I agree with you on that." Molders reply was smooth and soft. Even though he could not see him Domino could picture the man's face in his mind full of false concerns. How could Buck not see this man for what he truly was? "All I am saying sire is that much has changed over the years if Brutus-hay is to survive we must adapt with those changes perhaps you should think more on it later after your coronation."

Domino felt his anger growing what kind of a fool was Molder? Had not their mother warned him of what would happen if he tried to bring this kind of foolishness up again? Or did he just truly not think that the queen would follow thru with her threats.

He needed to bring an end to this conversation now! Without Buck or Molder knowing he had been listening. Making his way back to the stable entrance he called out. "Buck, if your hiding in here mother is looking for you again and she is not pleased I am not either, I have better things to do than look for you all the time. But if you don't want to be king or marry Shilo that's ok I will do it. Hell, she would proudly be happier with me anyway."

Bucks' voice rang out from the back of the stables. "Keep dreaming sugar britches you could never handle a woman like her."

"Right." Domino replied sarcastically "And you could." Not giving his brother a chance to respond he changed the subject "I heard voices when I came in who are you talking to?" He asked innocently.

Molder stepped out into the walkway before Buck could answer. "That would be me, Prince Domino the young king and I were just discussing the events of tomorrow. My apologies to the Queen if I kept him from his duties."

Domino had to try hard to keep the distrust he felt for this man show. Liar! he thought I heard what you said and I know what you are trying to do it won't happen as easily as you think I won't let you use my brother for your own needs.

"It is going to be a big day tomorrow," Domino said out loud "Will you be with us to greet Stormracer this time?"

Molder shook his head "Regrettably no, I will not be able to attend young prince I have pressing family matters away that I must deal with please give the good mare my apologies."

Heading for the stable door Buck stopped mid step. "But you missed the last greeting Molder it does not seem right that you should miss this one as well."

That was right Domino thought he was not at the last greeting. It was more than a little strange that someone in this man's position would twice not be there for such events. Kings traveled for thousands of miles hoping for a chance to meet the mare of legend. What family matter was so important that it could not be put off for one day, and why had Molder not talked about it before?

Smiling Molder put a hand on both of their shoulders and walked out of the stables with them. "I am an old man my young friends I have seen the great mare many times in my life. I will see her the next time. My only regret is that I will not be here to see you take the throne for the first time or to see you and the young Shilo be wed. Please accept my sincere apologies. Now we need to be going, after all, we must not keep your mother the queen waiting."

Shays voice rang out through the courtyard reaching even the farthest corners. "In the sight of God and with the power given to me by the people of this great land and the rulers of the past I seal this bond between the two of you as man and wife. Welcome both of you King Buck and Queen Shilo the new protectors and rulers of Brutus-hay, may God watch over you and guide your hands in caring for the people of this great land. Let the heavens and earth know that from this day forward the rains of leadership is handed down to my son Buck and his new wife Shilo. The new King and Queen of Brutus-hay!"

Domino's voice joined in with the thousands of others cheering the new King and Queen even amongst the defending cheers Domino could hear Stormracer's joyful whinny. Buck and Shilo looked both looked proud and embarrassed. Domino made his way over to the couple giving both of them a quick bow waiting Till he could be heard he told them, "And in the sight of God I pledge my life and loyalty to the new King and Queen of Brutus-hay."

"And I as well." Another voice echoed his beside him, glancing over Domino met his mother's eyes as she rose from a graceful curtsey.

"Thank you, both of you," Buck said. "I am counting on both of you to help me through this and let me know when I am wrong."

"Oh don't worry," Shay told him laughing. "When you need it we will set you straight."

"From time to time all wander from their path." Stormracer's voice sounded in their heads, "Whether a king or a wandering merchant it is good to have those you can trust to set you straight again. I as well offer my loyalty to the new king and queen of Brutus-hay." Stretching out a foreleg she lowered her muzzle to it in a graceful bow. "Long may you live and reign!" Lifting her head she let out another joyful whinny Domino found his self-joining in as the courtyard once more erupted with cheers.

For Domino, the rest of the day passed far too quickly, in all of Brutus-hays long history there had never been a day such as this and the people were determined to celebrate. Not even Stormracer was immune to the atmosphere going so far as to joke with the people. Domino was watching her as she summoned a small rain cloud over a drunk partygoer dousing the man before he could place an improper hand on unsuspecting women. Jumping back in shock the man spun around angrily to see who had thrown water on him only to stop when he saw the mare glaring at him. Like the other people watching Domino could not hear the mind send the mare sent, but it had a sobering effect on the man. Looking embarrassed and ashamed he apologized to the woman before leaving.

Making his way over to her Domino stopped as a familiar young girl came up to the mare with a stout dog trailing behind her "Excuse me, lady Stormracer." The young girl said shyly "Do you remember me from last time? I don't think I told you my name I'm Dottie"

Stormracer's ears flicked forward as she nickered a greeting to the nervous girl. "Of course, I remember you, child, it is good to see you again, you have grown into a very pretty young woman. And this is the sick pup from before is it not?"

"Yes, I named him Corkie I wanted to show him to you I hope that is ok." The girl blurted out.

"And why would it not be child?" Stormracer ask her softly

Looking more embarrassed than before at the growing crowd Dottie muttered "Well...You're Stormracer. And I am no one really...just a girl."

"We are both Gods children, I am no more or less than you, always remember that." Stormracer told her "None can help what they are born, it is how you live and the choices that you make in life that will be counted and yours is a kind and gentle soul," Dipping her head Stormracer went on "The day is not yet over I would be honored if you and Corkie would share the rest of it with me."

The day ended too soon for everyone and the courtyard filled once more to watch as Stormracer prepared to leave. Standing on the balcony she turned to face Buck and Shilo "None can change their destiny." She told them. "Our paths and trials were set for us long ago it is how you live and the choices that you make in life that will be counted." She told them repeating her earlier words meaningfully. "Both of you will face test in your lives, both with each other and in ruling this great land. In how you deal with your personal matters I can only tell you to trust in your love for one another. But in matters of the kingdom, there is one thing I can give that will one day help."

Lifting her head she let out a soft nicker Domino was reminded of a mare calling its foal. Everyone on the balcony jumped back as a flash of lighting flared then froze in place just over their heads.

Nicking again Stormracer's eyes flashed as storm clouds formed around the bolt of lightning huge and menacing flashing with smaller bolts of lightning of their own, a breeze sprang up quickly turning into a powerful gale tugging at the clothes of everyone in the courtyard and forcing the people closest to it on the balcony backward.

Bobbing her head and rearing on her hind legs the mare let out a loud whiny churning the air with her forefeet. Like a living thing the storm and wind started circling the mare drawing in ever closer Just when it looked like the storm would overwhelm her Stormracer brought her forelegs down with a thunderous crash shaking the castle itself, and with a bright flash of light, the storm was gone. Replaced by a small shimmering medallion set with three stones hovering in the air in front a surprised Buck.

"My gift to you young king, within this medallion, is the power of the hurricane, treat it with respect, Once unleashed you will only be able to control it for a very short time. There will be times when you will want to use it but understand, you must use it only as a last resort. And that time will come, young king, I cannot tell you when only that it will and when it does you will know."

Reaching out carefully Buck took the medallion "Thank you Good mare I promise to keep it safe and use it wisely."

Dipping her head Stormracer blew out softly "And once again I must leave you, farewell good king and queen may God guide your hands in ruling this land," Turning she leaped off the balcony and with a loud whiny to the people below galloped into the darkening sky.

Domino rode at the head of the column returning from what seemed like a never-ending meeting their northern neighbor King Mulkies the leader of Spiral. It had been five years since Buck and Shilo's wedding and in that time he had made eight trips to meet with the man who never seemed to miss a chance to tell anyone he could corner all about his personal body problems. At this point, he would almost be willing to go to war with the man just to get out of another meeting.

To add to his problems Nipper was starting to limp on her near forefoot. Pulling her to a stop he slid off the mare to inspect her leg. Lancer reined in beside him watching as he run his hand down her fetlock the area just above her ankle was starting to feel hot. "How bad is it?" he ask

Felling gently Domino grunted, "Just a pulled muscle I think, she stumbled a little ways back I didn't think she was hurt at the time she only started limping a few minutes ago. You take the men and head on home it's only a half day ride from here. There is a stream a few miles east of here I will lead her there and soak her leg for a bit the cold water will take the swelling down. When you get home send someone back with a fresh horse for me."

"There have been three raids by outlaws in this area in the last month and If you think that I am going to face your mother and tell her that I left you out here on your own your nuts." Lancer laughed "I know you can take care of yourself and you know it but I will be damned if I am going to stand in arms reach of that women and try to convince her that it was a good idea to just leave you out here. I want to live to see my grandchildren grow up. We will send the men ahead I am staying with you."

"Coward!" Domino said teasingly.

Lancer slid out of his saddle landing beside Domino, "When it comes to that woman you're damned right."

Straightening back up Domino patted the mare on the neck calling out to the captain of his escort."

"Bane, Nipper pulled a muscle, I am going to have to lead her to Brownie creek and soak her leg awhile Lancer will stay with me you take the rest of the men and head home let them know what happened."

Bane trotted Cyclone a large brown and white mare down the line of waiting men reining in next to the two. "Are you sure this is a good idea sire? The bandits have been more and more brazen lately, the patrols have driven them off three times in this area alone. Mayhap it would be best if we remained with you. I am sure that the king would rather receive a late report than lose a brother."

"We will be safe enough," Lancer said quickly. "I know a hidden route not far from here and there are some matters I wish to speak with the Prince about in private, personal matters." He added quickly before Bane could take offense. "And if you ride quickly you can reach the castle and be back with fresh horses before nightfall."

Still looking unsure Bane conceded. "Very well we will go then and be back as quickly as possible. I hope your personal matters are worth risking your lives for."

"We will be safe enough," Domino told him. "You watch out for yourselves a group as large as yours is easier seen than two man and the thieves may try an ambush. It would not be the first time."

"True." Bane said turning Cyclone. "But it would be the last for any that tried. I almost wish they would I would welcome a chance to rid this land of at least some of them."

"You said that there was something you wanted to talk about," Domino ask Lancer when the patrol was out of earshot.

"Yes," Lancer told him. "But I don't think you are going to like hearing what I have to tell you."

"I don't like a lot of things people tell me." Domino joked "But I have to listen anyway one of the pains of being a Prince or at least that is what mother keeps telling me."

Chuckling Lancer started leading Carter towards the distant stream. "True I suppose. What I tell you my friend cannot go beyond the two of us, at least not until we are sure of what I suspect."

"Go on." Domino told him, "Whatever it stays between us for now."

"Looking to make sure that no one else was around." Lancer spoke quietly "My Prince, I believe that Molder is somehow influencing the king!"

Domino kept his eyes on the trail ahead "Influencing him how?"

"Of that, I am not sure," Lancer told him. "But two moons ago I couldn't sleep so I went for a late night ride outside the city. I was riding on the north creek trail I like that route, not many folk travel it, too much brush. When I heard voices a first I thought it might be two lovers so I tried to sneak around them without disturbing them. Then I recognized the voices it was the King and Molder, I started to leave but I thought it strange that they would be meeting at such a time and place or I would have just left. Forgive me my friend I know it was wrong to listen in on your brother but I think you should know what was being said."

Domino nodded. "Go on," he told Lancer.

Looking uncomfortable Lancer continued. "I did not hear what was being said at first, but when I got closer." Lancer hesitated. "Domino I know that Molder was your father's friend, and I have no wish to ruin our friendship so trust me I would not be telling you this if I did not think it was important."

"Molder was my father's friend and Buck listens to him but I myself have no love for the man," Domino told him. "Whatever you have to tell me, do so.'

Looking relieved Lancer went on. "Sire I heard him telling the king that the kingdom would be better off if we tamed Stormracer!"

Domino stopped dead in his tracks. "Tamed Stormracer?" He snapped. "Are you sure that is what he said tame her?"

Seeming taken aback "Yes." Lancer answered "I am positive I was not sure I heard right at first but he said it more than once, in fact, he kept saying it. That is what struck me as odd, at first the king was just as upset as you but every time that Molder repeated himself your brother seemed less and less upset about it. Like he was in a trance of some kind. I thought about interrupting them somehow but I was not sure how the king would react in his state and if with no one else there it would be my word against Molders. I don't know for sure that your brother even knew what was happening."

"And if Molder is somehow influencing Buck you would be hard passed to get anyone to listen to you." Domino finished for him. "Still you should have come to me with this sooner if Molder is planning something there is no knowing how far he has got!" Glaring it the distant mountains he muttered, "I need to get home! I am sorry to ask you this my friend but I need Carter can you get Nipper home safe on your own?"

"If you are worried about the thieves roaming around, I would almost hope to run into them but if we stick to the creek we should be fine. From what I have heard there have been no sightings in that area. Are you sure you will be alright with Carter? He is a somewhat different type of horse than most."

"If by that you mean he is not in his right mind." Domino muttered, "Everyone already knows that. But yes I am pretty sure I can handle him. Not that I have much choice right now anyway." He added swinging up on the big gray and white horse. Carter stood stiff as Domino mounted lunging forward as soon as Domino made contact with the saddle jerking the reins he got control of the stallion patting his neck to calm him. "As soon as I reach the castle I will send riders back for you till then try to stay out of sight." Booting Carter in the side he turned the horse and raced for home. It was a half day ride to the castle at a normal pace Domino and Carter made it in a third of that time the stallion never wanting to go slower than a fast trot Domino had to keep a tight rein on the stud to make him walk.

"Calm down horse," Domino told him patting his sweaty neck. "I want this ride to be over as much as you do for a different reason I am sure, but it will do neither of us any good if you pull up lame too." Carter pulled on the bit in answer.

"Honestly horse." Domino growled, "I have never seen anyone lay a hard hand on you, the way you act one would think that you had been beaten your whole life." Snorting Carter relaxed his pace seeming to realize that he was not going to win this debate. Warily letting the reins go slack Domino sat back in the saddle walking the horse to give him time to cool and catch his breath as they rode out of the foothills into the valley below. Topping the last rise Domino could see the distant outline of the city and castle the road leading to it stretched out before it like a long black snake.

Stopping to let Carter rest Domino noticed movement on the road coming out of the city. Even at this distance, he could tell it was a column of men riding fast. Straining his eyes to the limit he tried to make out what was happening finally giving up. They were too far away but one thing was certain for so many men to be riding that hard something was wrong, spurring Carter he raced to intercept the fast-moving column of men.

As he got closer he saw that his first guess was right something was very wrong. Coming down the road at a canter was Buck riding Noose a little black and white mare at the head of a column of over five hundred heavily armed men. Angling Carter toward his brother Domino fell in beside him. The grim look on Bucks' face pushed any doubt out of his mind. "What is happening?" He asked.

Bucks tight-lipped answer sent a cold shiver down his spine. "Mother has been taken by thieves, she went out with her escort this morning like she always does and never made it back. They were ambushed in Silver valley all her escort was killed. A farmer saw it happen and rode to tell us, the last he saw of her they had taken her captive. We are going after them to get her back and put an end to this and them once and for all even if it means chasing them through every kingdom in the lands! I swear if they harm her……..!" Choked with emotion Bucks voice trailed off.

"I'm going with you." Domino told him, "But I need a fresh horse."

Looking back along the line of men Buck called out to one of the younger men, breaking line the man brought his horse up beside them. "Yes, sire."

Nodding at Domino, "Dread, I know you want as much as any of us to rescue my mother, But I need you to switch mounts with Domino. Take his back to the city and see he is properly cared for. If you can get a fresh horse and catch up to us do it, but don't get yourself or the horse killed trying, understand?"

"Yes, sire" The young man said not able to keep the disappointment out of his voice.

Guiding their horses to the side of the dirt road the two men traded mounts as the column rode by. "Her name is Crickett, my lord." Dread told him, "She is young and still a little green but she is strong and listens she will do you well."

Thanking him Domino traded horses with the young soldier, "There is something more I need you to do." Domino told him, "Nipper pulled up lame and I left Lancer with her at Brownie creek about forty miles from here. Can you take some men and an extra horse and see that he gets back safely?"

Looking in the direction of the departing column of men Dread sighed, "Yes my prince, with all haste." The young man started to turn Carter towards the city then stopped.

"When I was younger I fell playing. Queen Shay saw and stopped what she was doing to help me up and bandage my scrapped arm with a sleeve torn from her dress, I still have that bandage, and your mother is a good woman I hope she has not been harmed."

"As do I." Domino told him turning Cricket, "When we get her back you should find her and let her know you remember what she did, she would like that"

Catching up to the column Domino rode to the lead beside his brother. "I've sent scouts ahead to track them." Buck told him "From what reports we have heard they have been striking mostly in the southern part of the kingdom, I am betting that they have a camp there. I should have sent a garrison of men to find them and wipe them out years ago. I didn't that was a mistake, I just pray that mother does not pay for it."

"It's not your fault brother." Domino told him, "Mother went out every morning, never by the same route though, the thieves must have spotted them and set up an ambush." That or someone told them what road she would be taking, He thought but who? A dark suspicion filled his mind angrily he scanned the riders behind them. "Where is Molder? Does he know what happened?"

Buck gave him a funny look, "Molder? He is back at the castle I suppose I am not sure if he knows what happened or not. Why would we bring an old man to a battle?"

Feeling foolish Domino answered grudgingly, "I did not mean take him into battle I was just wondering if he had been told yet."

"I am sure he knows by now." Buck said turning his attention back to the road. "The whole city saw us ride out and you can bet that everyone has heard by now."

For the next twenty miles, they rode in silence speaking only when they had to, No one felt like talking. Concern and fear for the queen showing in everyone's eyes.

Lost in his own thoughts Domino was startled when Buck tapped him on the shoulder. "Wake up brother, I ask if you thought it would be a good idea to go around Lonesome Canyon or ride through, it would be faster to go through but it is also a good place for an ambush. "The long line of men behind them stopped as the two brothers consulted.

Following his brothers gaze Domino studied the canyon, "I say ride through I know it is a risk but it will take longer to ride around every second we delay puts mother in greater danger. Besides if the thieves were setting an ambush there the scouts would have warned us by now."

Nodding his head in agreement Buck nudged Noose ahead down the canyon path. They had barely taken a step when grunting Buck brought the mare to a stop. "Looks like we are going to get an answer to that question now." Lifting a hand he pointed as several men road out of the canyon at a dead gallop. "There are the scouts now."

Spotting them the scouts raced up bringing their horses to a sliding stop. Domino did not have to hear what the men had to say to know they did not carry good news. As Skyblue reined his sweat-soaked horse in beside them the man's face was grim as he tried to calm the blowing horse. "Sire, we found their camp about five miles off, there are about four hundred men they look to be well armed but not very disciplined."

"And what of our mother is she with them?" Buck ask

Dropping his eyes Sky Blue answered hesitantly. "I saw her my king she is alive but…."

"But what?!" Buck snapped, "Damn it this is no time for games! Is my mother alright?"

"She is alive, but they are not treating her well." Skyblue said softly lifting his head to meet Bucks angry eyes."

"Not treating her well?" Buck echoed Skyblue's words darkly. Domino felt the fury building in his own chest there was no doubting the meaning behind the guard's words

"I am sorry my king, we wanted to ride in to help her but they have too many men for just the few of us to go against. We thought it best to find you and lead you to them."

Glaring at the man Buck spurred Noose ahead racing off at a gallop. Slapping Crickett's flank with the reins Domino caught up to his brother pulling the mares head around in front of Noose forcing her to a stop. "Buck wait! Think, we can't just go charging in without a plan we will get mother killed for sure."

"I have a plan!" Buck snarled "We are going to ride in kill all of them and free mother and God help anyone who gets in our way!" Pulling on Noose reins Buck tried to guide the horse past Domino and Cricket."

"Great plan brother." Domino snapped back, "And which one of us is going to bury mother after we get her killed? Dammit, You're a king think like one, and not some hot headed fool."

Fury flared behind Bucks' eyes and for a minute Domino thought that his brother was going to strike him. Then he relaxed as he saw the anger fade. Closing his eyes for a brief second Buck opened them again staring hard at his younger brother. "Fine, you are right we need a plan, I take it you have one?"

Nodding his head Domino turned to Skyblue who had caught up to them waiting with the rest of the men. "Tell me about their camp, how hard would it be to surround them and have they posted guards?"

Domino studied thieves' camp intently looking for any sign of Shay the sun had sat by the time they had found it and put their plan in place but the large fires light up the camp and the dirty tents with their flickering light. Feeling a touch on his shoulder he half turned startled. "Relax Brother it is just me." Buck whispered, "Have you spotted mother yet?"

"No..." Domino stopped mid-sentence as the flap of the main tent below was shoved open faint laughter reached them from inside the tent as a half-naked woman was shoved out to land face first in the mud. Followed by a large heavy set man pulling on his shirt. Pushing herself up with her arms the woman's face was light up by the firelight. Domino had to restrain himself from charging into the camp in a mindless rage when he recognized her, Queen Shay his mother.

Hearing Bucks furious hiss he grabbed his brother's arm as he lunged forward. "Wait, I want them dead to brother but remember the plan, we have to give Skyblue and the rest of the men time to get in place."

Reluctantly Buck stopped, "Fine we wait, but that man is mine Domino, understand? I want him!"

Keeping his eyes on Shay Domino nodded grimly, "You want him, brother he is yours, I will get mother out of there, just don't get careless."

Both brothers watched as another man exited the tent behind the first the second one putting his foot against Shays back as she tried to get up forcing her back into the mud. "Stay where you belong slut, you might have been a queen in your city but here you are nothing but a whore."

Rolling over onto her back Shay glared at the men her voice dripping with contempt. "To be a whore I would need a man, and as of yet I have not seen one among you."

Grabbing her by the hair the second man pulled her up unsheathing a dagger from his side. "You're a proud slut I will give you that, let's see if I can't help you get rid of some of that arrogance." Pulling her head around, the man started hacking at her long hair. Shay brought her knee up with blinding speed even from where the brothers were hiding they could hear the impact when it made contact with the man's groin.

Dropping both the dagger and Shay the man fell sideways groaning. Landing on her feet she made a grab for the dagger only to stagger sideways as a backhanded blow from the heavier of the two men caught her alongside her head stunning her and knocking her back into the mud. Before she could move again two more men grabbed her arms and drug her back to her feet.

"I will wait no longer!" Buck snarled, lunging to his feet Buck charged the camp with Domino close behind neither of the brothers knew for sure if Skyblue and the rest of their patrol were ready and neither cared. The only thing that mattered was helping their mother and if that meant fighting the whole band of thieves alone that was what they meant to do.

Keeping to the shadows till the last minute the two charged the men ringing the campfire. Not expecting an attack of any kind were caught off guard, most of them had been watching their leaders and Shay next to the fire not even knowing they were under attack until it was too late. Domino never slowed his pace as he cut the closest man's legs out from under him using the momentum from the swing he twisted around to bury his sword in the chest of the next man who was just starting to draw his sword.

A third man swung his sword wildly in Domino's direction his eyes still not adjusted to the night darkness after looking across the fire. Domino jumped back from the swing drawing and throwing his dagger in the same movement catching the man in the throat. Looking over at Buck he saw his brother finishing off the other three men at the fire. When a harsh voice sounded from across the fire, "Make one more move either of you and she dies!"

Looking across the fire Dominos felt a cold knot in his stomach standing just inside the light of the fire was his mother the heavy sit man standing behind her a knife to her throat and a man on each side of her holding her arms tight.

Reluctantly both Buck and Domino stopped their advance. "Let her go now." Buck spat from between clenched teeth, "And you have my word that we will not come looking for you or your men till morning, we will give you that much of a head start." Ignoring Domino's shocked look Buck went on. "Do it and you have that much chance to live, but if you lay one more hand on her I promise you I will personally skin the three of you alive!"

Pulling against the men holding her arms Shay yelled across the fire at her sons "Don't try to deal with this filth Buck their word means nothing kill them now and rid the land of them for good!"

Grabbing Shay's hair from behind the heavy sit men pulled her head back exposing her throat and the razor sharp knife pushed against it to the light, a trickle of blood was starting to run down her neck where the two met. "Such bitterness from a lady and Queen."

He said mockingly "Not what an undisciplined piece of filth like myself would expect from royalty still full of arrogance you would think that sharing our bed would have taken some of that out of her would you not?"

Domino could feel his rage building more with each one of the man's words from the corner of his eye he could see Bucks hands trembling it was taking every ounce of strength both of them had not to charge the men but movement from the edges of the fire told him that the rest of the camp had heard the commotion and had come to investigate.

Dammit, he thought what was taking the others so long? If the two of them attacked alone now they would only get their mother killed. And he was not sure how much longer Buck could restrain himself or me as well he thought seeing his mother like this...

"To be honest I was not expecting you so quickly." The heavyset man told them. "When we took the old queen here we made sure that there were no witnesses I thought we would have at least one more day before we saw any pursuit." Shrugging he muttered, "Not that it really matters, We were going to send you a ransom demand in the morning anyway just thought it would be fun to keep her for a night if you know what I mean." he added leeringly, "In fact this makes things easier we had our fun and you saved us the trouble of having to send a messenger.

Of course one would expect more of a rescue party then just two men," looking into the darkness he muttered, "And there is more than just the two of you is there not? The others are out there waiting for your signal. Like I said not that it really matters if you want the old queen here to live that is. Now listen carefully and do exactly what I tell you, little king, if you want your mother to live. I know that the storm mare gave you an amulet, one of great power you wear it around your neck now do you not?"

Looking across at his brother Domino could see the golden chain around his neck that held the medallion. As far as he knew Buck had never taken it off but how would this man know that? Everyone that was there on the day of the coronation knew that Stormracer had given it to him, but only a very few knew that Buck never parted with it. Reaching up with a hand to touch the medallion under his shirt Buck met his brother's eyes Domino could see the same question going through his mind.

Chuckling the big man held out his hand, "Don't bother to answer I know you have it and I want it. Very carefully take it off and toss it over here do anything else and I promise you will watch her die in front of you." Reaching into his shirt with his free hand Buck lifted the chain over his head and held it out in front of him the medallion twisting slowly on the end of the chain.

"NO!" Shay spat, "Buck don't give it to him my life is not worth it!"

Before anyone could reply the medallion caught the light from the fire suddenly flaming with a light of its own filling the camp with a blinding light. Shay recovered first moving before anyone pulling free of her captors and grabbing a sword from the nearest men's belt. Spinning around she sliced it threw the startled man's neck and into the second man's chest in one movement.

Still moving she grabbed a second sword off the ground and leaped across the fallen man's body at their heavyset leader. Yells rang out from across the fire and Domino was still seeing spots in front of his eyes as he tried to make out what was happening, the area around the large fire was full of men. Bringing his sword around in a backhanded swing he stopped mid swing as a familiar voice yelled his name. "Hold Prince Domino, it is me"

Blinking away the last of the spots he recognized the speaker. "Skyblue, what took so long?"

"My apologies my friend I will explain later after we get your mother to safety." The young guard yelled over his shoulder as he ran into the mass of man and blades.

Looking around Domino spotted Buck fighting with two men on the edge of the fire running he grabbed the closest of the two bringing the butt of his sword hard against the side of the man's head feeling the man's skull give way. Dropping the limp body he grabbed Bucks arm, "Where is mother? I lost track of her"

Desperately both brothers searched the ongoing battle "Domino!" Buck shouted pointing "Over there, she's over there!" Turning to follow his brothers gaze Domino's heart stopped when he saw his mother half naked without any armor in the middle of the battle facing off against the larger heavy set leader.

Both brothers lunged into the fray trying to fight their way through the battle to their mother's side. To Domino it seemed like the entire battle was moving in slow motion the ground seemed to pull at his feet and no matter how many men that fell more seemed to take their place. The knot of fear for his mother growing with each passing heartbeat as the battle grew more and more intense.

Domino could not help but remember Lancer's words during their training exercises, "There are few people in the lands that I would not go up against in battle. Your mother, Queen Shay is one of them. If you get the chance to, study her when she is practicing watch how she moves she never waste a motion she is the most deadly fighter I have ever seen."

Watching her now Domino understood what he was talking about. Even though her opponent was far bigger it was clear that it was Shay that had the upper hand her every movement flowed effortlessly into the next. Pressing the men further back with every swing till tripping on a hidden tree root the men stumbled backward giving her the opening she needed. Moving quickly she lunged forward shoving her sword into the man's chest.

Small bands of fighting were still going on but the battle was dying down with most of the thieves either having run off or dead. Buck and Domino were making their way to Shay with the fighting all but over she leaned tiredly against a tree looking small and worn nothing like the woman they had just witnessed in battle. Seeing her sons she straightened up with a smile.

"My rescuers…" With a look of shock, Shay fell sideways an arrow sticking out of the side of her chest. Hearing a yell from behind a large patch of briars Domino saw a rider racing off on horseback with three guardsmen in pursuit

Jumping Forward Buck grabbed his falling mother gently laying her on the ground. Pulling off his shirt Domino folded it quickly and laid it on the ground beneath her head. Shay let out a soft gasp as Buck run a probing hand around the arrow shaft sticking out the side her chest. "Don't!" Domino said grabbing his brother's hand. "If we pull it out we could make it worse." Looking up at the men who were starting to gather around he yelled, "We need a healer now!"

"I was not going to pull it out, brother." Buck snapped "Do you really take me for that much of a fool? I was just trying to see for sure what angle the arrow took!" Tearing off a strip of cloth off his own shirt Buck gently wiped the blood from around their mother's mouth.

Shay opened her half-closed eyes focusing them on her sons. "My rescuers," she coughed. "I am so proud of both of you." Shays small body shook with another harsh cough.

Wiping the bubbling blood from around her mouth again Buck laid the back of his hand gently alongside her face. "Shhh, mother please don't try to talk you will only make it worse everything is going to be alright I promise you I can fix this. A healer will do her no good," Buck said grimly "The arrow passed through both lungs, she is dying there is only one who can save her."

Domino watched confused as Buck got to his feet and made his way through the ring of watching men walking past the last of the men Buck lifted his face to the sky, "I Buck king of Brutus-hay as granted by the laws and rights of the land, call to you great mare in this time of need I summon you, hear me and answer!" Lowering his head he whispered "Please."

Hundreds of eyes searched the sky worriedly as at first only silence answered Bucks plea. Domino watched as his brother made a slow circle turning in place watching hopefully before dropping his head in defeat. "Please." he repeated Tears starting at the corners of his eyes.

Feeling a touch on his arm Domino looked down at his mother, Shays' eyes glowed with joy as she pointed over her son's shoulder at the eastern sky. At first, he could see only the night stars but suddenly realized that the lowest one was growing fast in size. Standing quickly he pointed, "Buck over there, She heard you she is coming!"

Relief filled Bucks eyes as he made his way back through the watching men to his mother's side. Moving fast across the sky the light grew larger until the entire valley was lit with a midnight sun. Then hovering in place above their heads the light collapsed in on itself leaving a familiar form in its place. Stormracer's voice echoed sadly in everyone's heads. "You have called good king and I have come but I know what it is you want to ask of me. I am truly sorry but I cannot grant you what you wish. I cannot heal your mother."

"What!" Buck yelp "Why not? I don't understand I saw you save a pups life. What reason could there be that you would let her suffer and die like this?"

Hovering above the group's heads Stormracer looked down at Buck with sorrowful eyes. "The pup's life had only just begun. I did nothing but take the illness from his body it was God that decided that he should continue in this life, not me. Shay has traveled the trails and trials of this life and reached their end. God has decided that it is time for her to be reunited with Dragon I cannot and will not try to work against God's will.

For her sons and the kingdom, I am truly sorry and I mourn your loss. But understand this should not be a sorrowful day but one of joy, Queen Shay will be rejoining King Dragon in Gods lands for all of eternity." As she was speaking Stormracer slowly settled lower and lower till her hooves were on the ground both Buck and Domino stepped back to make room for her next to Shay. Looking down at the women Stormracer's voice softened even more "It is time good women, are you ready?"

Weakly Shay nodded her head, lowering her muzzle close to the dying woman Stormracer let out a soft nicker. Domino heard soft mutters of disbelief from the group of surrounding men as Shays body went limp and a soft light slowly rose above it. Reaching the mares back the light expanded outwards with a flash Dominos breath caught in his throat when the twinkling form on Stormracer's back looked at him with proud eyes and he heard his mother's voice in his head. "Do not blame yourselves and do not mourn me, my son's. Stormracer is right it is merely my time, I know you will miss me as I have Dragon. But I will never stop loving you and I will be with you always, remember that and watch out for each other. We will be together again in time." Reaching out Shay patted Stormracer on the neck with a ghostly hand and with a graceful leap the mare climbed above the trees and disappeared into the night sky.

A heavy silence hung over the men gathered around Shays body every eye watching the fading light of the mare carrying the queen to her reunion with Dragon. Watching the light twinkle and fade Domino lay a hand on Bucks' shoulder. 'Brother we need to get mother home the people have to be told."

Numbly Buck nodded, "Get her home," He echoed turning to his brother he whispered, "I failed her brother I let her die."

"No!" Domino snapped "You did not, this was not your fault Buck! None of it, like Stormracer told us it was mother's time. .I will miss her just as much as you but I am not going to spend the rest of my life blaming myself or pointing fingers at others that is not what our mother would want." Sighing he gazed at the slowly lighting sky. "She is with father now and they are happy that is how I am going to think of it and how you should as well brother.”

Running a hand through his hair Buck nodded, “You are right they are together now and we should be happy for them. But life is not going to be the same without her Domino not ever again.”

The news of Shay’s death traveled quickly and within two days the city streets crowded full with travelers from far off lands who had come to honor her. Even the furthest lands sent carrier birds with messages of condolence. Domino couldn't help but feel proud to think that his mother was so well thought of. As was the costume queen Shays body was laid to rest in a graveyard on the hillside at the edge of the great gardens.

The gentle rise of the hill was lined with the grave markers of the kings and queens of the past. Domino and Buck stood in silence side by side next to the last and newest one in the line when à familiar voice interrupted their thoughts. “Forgive the intrusion my friends but I must be returning back to my duties in the morning and I wanted to speak to you before I departed.” Both brothers recognized the speaker King Mulkies. “I am truly sorry for your loss, your mother was a truly special women all of the lands will be lessened by her passing, and my life will be that much emptier as well. Your mother was one of the few people willing to tolerate my stories.”

Mulkies gave the brothers à rueful grin “I know very well what people say of me and to be honest I do not care, but Queen Shay was the most tolerant person I ever met. Her kindness to me and my people will never be forgotten, I give you both my word as King of my lands that the people of Bruits Hay will always be welcome in my home and my kingdom.”

More than à little embarrassed by how he had spoken of the man in the past Buck dipped his head in a respectful nod. “Thank you, my friend, I hope it never comes to that but we will remember your offer.”

“And if there is anything you or your people need.” Domino added, “You need only to ask.”

Mulkies held out a friendly hand grasping Dominos. “As it has always been, Thank you. Now if you will excuse me I must be off, the journey home is à long one and I feel the need to relieve myself of excess gas.”

Watching the man deport Buck muttered, “At least he gave us a warning, I feel sorry for the people he is traveling with though."

Brutus-hay never had much of a winter and what they did have seldom lasted long, this year that had changed as if the land itself was mourning Shay's death. Domino was returning from what seemed like an endless journey from the lands northern borders. Buck had signed a trade pact with their northern neighbors and as the chief ambassador, it had fallen on Domino to work out the details that always seemed to minor for a king to bother with. Not long ago that would have annoyed him to no end and he would have been quick to set his brother straight but lately, he had greater worries on his mind.

For almost a year after Shays death, the kingdom was peaceful the thieves that were not killed in the battle ether fled or went into hiding. To Domino the castle seemed far more cold and empty, Buck had changed since their mother's funeral even though he tried to hide it was clear that he never got over blaming himself for his mother's death. That worried Domino, more than once he tried to talk to his brother about it but it was near impossible to get him alone it seemed that Molder never left his brothers side. And the rumors he was hearing from those within earshot of the two only added to his distrust of the man. Molder seemed to sense Domino's dislike for him staying as far away from him as possible having no love for the man he was fine with that. But if even half of the rumors he was hearing about what Molder was whispering in Bucks' ears were true then he had to put a stop to it, now!

Riding Nipper through the wide stable doors he was glad to be out of the worst of the wind and cold, as one of the grooms pulled the stable doors shut behind the last guardsman, Domino slid out of the saddle almost collided with Shilo as she came running up to him the look of fear in her eyes told him what words could not. "Domino you have to talk to Buck, I tried to make him listen to reason but Molder has done something to him he won't listen to me he might listen to you, he is in the courtyard now with Molder and several of the city guardsmen. The last week he has had them trying to catch Stormracer."

Handing Nipper's rains to a waiting groom Domino gently grabbed Shilo's shoulders trying to calm her, "Easy, slow down, what do you mean trying to catch her? I know that Molder has made foolish comments before about such things, but it can't be done. There is no rope or net made that can hold her and no mortal horse has any hope of catching her, she crosses the horizon as easily as a normal horse crosses a pasture."

Shaking free of his grip Shilo stepped back pointing in the direction of the courtyard. "Damn it Domino! Do you think I would be here like this now if there was nothing to worry about? Buck is getting ready to call her now! Molder used a spell he said he found in an old scroll to weave a net. It is not made out of rope he wove it with some kind of dark light he called up, he said it was starlight but I don't believe that. I heard the spell and I saw him weave the net Domino, it terrifies me it is evil, you have to stop them!"

Grabbing Shilo's hand Domino ran back through the stable doors in the direction of the courtyard. Glancing back at Shilo, "Has Molder spelled Buck somehow? I can't believe he would be doing this freely."

Fighting to keep her balance on the icy ground Shilo panted, "I don't know what he has done to Buck for sure I don't think it is a spell it is something else. Sometimes Buck acts fine other times it is like he is in a dream. He has gotten worse this last fortnight right after you left, I should have said something before but I thought it was just him blaming himself for your mother's death so I stayed silent."

"Don't blame yourself for this it is my fault as well I saw it happening several years ago but I never said anything I thought it was just my dislike of Molder making me see things," Domino told her as they reached the courtyard gate. "I should have put an end to that man years ago."

Running thru the garden gate the pair slowed to a fast walk searching the garden for Buck and Molder. "There!" Shilo said pointing to the fountain in the center of the gardens several Guardsmen and curious townsfolk were gathered watching Buck and Molder. "I can see them we're too late Buck has called her." Following Shilo's gaze Domino could see a fast-growing light on the horizon moving their way, Buck had called and Stormracer was coming.

With Shilo in tow Domino made his way through the crowded to the fountain were Buck and Molder were standing. Letting go of Shilo's hand he stepped between the two, facing Buck "You ordered the guards to try to catch Stormracer, have you gone insane?" Domino snapped "You know as well as I do brother that it is forbidden for any mortal man to touch her she is meant to run in Gods lands not the pastures of this world. And we both well know the price to be paid if any man were foolish enough to try to hold her." Looking over his shoulder at Molder he added darkly, "I don't know what you have been told since I left brother, but call this off!! Please come back with me to the castle. We can discuss this better after we both have had a night sleep and a meal under our belts."

Looking confused Buck stepped back from Domino. "I never ordered the guards to catch Stormracer…" He muttered shaking his head tiredly, "Molder what he is talking about?"

Watching Molder Domino felt an overwhelming distrust for this man Shilo was right somehow he was clouding Bucks mind. And without knowing for sure what Molder had done to his brother he ran a great risk of making matters worse by confusing him he had to find a way to make Buck see what was going on.

Smiling at Domino Molder spoke dismissively, "You are much like your mother she was stuck in the foolish ways of old too. Tales for children, no more, a horse is a horse wither they run through the pasture or in the sky, they are animals nothing more brute's meant to serve men." Sneering he looked over the garden walls at the quickly growing light. "But," He added mockingly." If the mare is truly one of God's animals as you say then you have nothing to fear surely he will protect her." Moving before anyone could stop him he threw out his hands in a swirling gesture. Jumping at the man Domino was knocked back by a blast of heat and flame as a glowing ball of flames shot forward engulfing the mare as she passed over the top of the garden walls.

Falling backward Domino felt someone grab him from behind stopping his fall and helping him back on his feet. Looking up he saw Buck helping him up and staring at something on the ground a looking confused and uncertain. Shilo stood next to her husband with several guardsmen and townspeople standing behind them all with the same shocked and frightened looks on their faces. Getting his feet back under him he turned already sure of what he was going to see.

The garden fountain stood with frozen icicles running down its rocky sides the normally green grass and trees covered with a light dusting of snow. Just the other side of the gardens a large glowing ball lay on the ground. Domino's heart stopped when the animal inside raised its head to look at them through the glowing ropes that made up the net. Stormracer!

Several of the guardsmen and townspeople rushed forward to try to cut the mare free. "No!" Domino yelled "Don't, if you touch her then nothing can help her." Drawing his sword he spun on Molder, "Free her now! Or I swear you will never see the morning sun."

Molder stepped back out of reach of Dominos sword with a taunting smile on his face "I did nothing but what the good king ask of me. He wanted the mare and I have given her to him." Pointing at the tangled mare he laughed. "If you don't believe look for yourself."

Keeping a wary eye on Molder Domino glanced behind him. Like a man sleepwalking Buck made his way to the glowing net. Stopping suddenly when Stormracer lifted her head to look at him. Even from where he was standing Domino could see the look of love and pity in her eyes as she watched Buck. Blowing softly Stormracer flicked her ears as a breezy voice echoed in the heads of everyone gathered close. "Good king, I know you have hoped and dreamed that one day we could race together across the skies as a child you prayed for it, asking God to allow it. And if it was possible I would do so joyfully, but it is not. God cannot allow it, not because he doesn't love his children but because we are of two different realms, such is the law and God will not break his own laws. When the time comes child for you to enter into God's lands I will carry you there with great pride. But now is not that time. Please, I know you do not act on your own accord."

Looking past Buck at Molder she went on. "Others have clouded your mind and I forgive you. But you must see past the darkness and free me, not for my sake but for the people of Brutus-hay. God lets me bring life and bounty to this land please, do not take that away."

Walking over to Buck Domino stepped between him and the trapped mare, "Brother please listen to her she speaks the truth, and mother warned us both about what would happen if anyone tried to hold Stormracer." Glaring over at Molder he snapped. "She tried to warn us about people like that fool who would tell us otherwise. Whatever he has told you it is wrong you know in your heart it is wrong, we have to free her before it is too late."

Moving around Domino Molder put a hand on Bucks arm, "Pay him no mind sire it is like I told you he is like all the others so willing to believe that a horse can control the weather, bring rain make the crops grow, foolish child tales sire she is just a horse nothing more a mare who would make a wonderful addition to the royal herds as breeding stock"

Shaking his head Buck pulled free from Molder's grip. '"What?" he stuttered, "A broodmare? What are you talking about?" Looking around at the gathered crowd he spotted the glowing net with the watching mare trapped inside. "Stormracer?!" Buck yelled spinning on Molder, "What is happening? What have you done? Free her Molder now! I told you before this is not what I wanted, free her! As your king I command it!"

Laughing Molder stepped away from Buck "You command me, little King? You have no idea who you speak to I have tolerated you and your parent's weakness only because it suited my needs but thankfully that time is past." Still talking Molder made his way to where Stormracer was lying tangled in the net Domino could see à dark aurora clinging to him growing brighter with every step he took. "You should thank me fool I have given you what you wanted but if you no longer wish to have the stormnag all you have to do is cut her free from the net," Waving à hand in the trapped horses' direction Molder taunted Buck, "Go ahead your majesty I won't try to stop you set her free"

Snarling Buck drew his dagger. "Guards hold him where he stands, I don't care who you are demon but I know you will pay for your crimes." Moving quickly the guards circled the grinning Molder who was watching Buck with gloating eyes as he kneeled next to the trapped mare. Carefully Buck pulled the glowing net away from Stormracer's flank, a sudden realization hit Domino leaping forward he yelled a warning, "Buck no, the spell!"

Without warning the net shot forwarded wrapping around Bucks hand pulling him in with the trapped mare as the glowing net suddenly burst into a dark ball of cold fire. Helpless Domino could only watch as his brother and Stormracer seemed to melt into each other. "No!" Shilo yelled racing past Domino her own dagger drawn in an attempt to free both her husband and Stormracer.

Grabbing her from behind Domino held back the struggling woman. 'It is too late if you try to free them you will only be trapped as well,"

"You don't know that!" Shilo screamed, "We can't just stand here watching we have to save them!" Sobbing she struggled in Dominos arms as the burning fire finally died down leaving behind two unmoving shapes.

Releasing Shilo, Domino stared in shock at the closest of the two. Barely moving his clothes burned off his body by the cold flames Buck lay face down on the snow lying just on the other side of him was Stormracer's unmoving form. Shilo hurried to his side putting a fearful hand on his shoulder she shook him gently "Buck, Buck, are you alright, what happened?"

Using his elbows to push himself up Buck lifted his head blinking his eyes dazedly like a man coming out of a deep sleep. Letting out a surprised gasp Shilo quickly backed away from the man she loved, looking at his brother Domino understood why. Except for his clothes being burned off his body Buck was untouched by the flames, with one very obvious difference. His eyes normally green now burned with an inner fire.

Rolling onto his back Buck gasp weakly. "Forget about me I will be ok, help Stormracer!"

Shilo unsnapped the clips on her heavy cloak wrapping it around Buck who was starting to shiver from the cold.

Domino and several of the guardsmen hurried to Stormracer's unmoving form. Reaching the mare first Daisy one of the few women in the city elite guard stopped a look of sheer horror on her face. "No," she gasp dropping on her knees in shock repeating herself over and over "No, please God no," Bane stood next to her with a hand on her shoulder the same look of horror in his eyes. Reaching them Domino saw the reason for their reaction. The Stormracer that had for millennia had run freely across the morning sky was gone were she had lay only moments ago now a statue a perfect copy of the beautiful mare formed interiorly of a single gleaming diamond lay in her place.

With Shilo's help Buck Got to his feet staring in disbelief at the frozen form of the mare even in the dim light of the moon it glowed with thousands of miniature stars of its own. With a savage snarl, he spun around pushing through the guards to where Molder stood unconcerned a taunting sneer on his face. "Why so angry little King, is this not what you wanted, are you not the fool who spent countless hours as a child watching on the hillsides in the chance that you might get to see her, praying for the day you could one day touch her? You should thank me I have given you that, rejoice! You have done what no mortals ever has or ever will do again."

. Grabbing à sword from the nearest guards hand Buck pushed the razor sharp tip against Molders throat. "Release her damn you whatever it is your spell did undo it. Or I will send you back to whatever Gods you worship in pieces."

Laughing Molder grabbed the sword blade dark foul smelling blood ran down its length as he twisted it free from Buck's hand and flung it over the garden wall. "Fool you still do not understand what has happened do you? Even if I wanted to I could not undo this, it was your hand not mine that cursed this land your hand that trapped the storm nag for eternity." A strong wind blew through the garden past the watching crowd.

Cold at first but warming quickly as it went, melting the snow and unfreezing the fountain. Waving an arm at the melting snow Molder taunted Buck, "Take a last look at your kingdom little king remember it for what it was and will never be again you will have all eternity to hold on to those memories. You see fool what you still do not understand in your ignorance is by touching the storm mare you not only trapped her but yourself as well. Only the smallest of slivers of her life force passed into you but more than enough to grant you eternal life to rule your new kingdom."

Watching the man Domino realized that like the snow Molders form seemed to be melting into the ground lunging he grabbed for the man only to have his hand pass through the misty shape. The man's taunting laughter and voice still echoed strong. "Live well little king rejoice in your new kingdom you will have all of time to rule over it, All hail King Buck ruler of the once great land of Brutus-hay! Once a kingdom of riches its people numbering in the tens of thousands soon to be a kingdom of one!" with the last word Molder vanished leaving only a dark stain on the ground where he had been standing.

Looking defeated Buck stared at the spot where Molder had been standing, walking up to her husband Shilo put a comforting hand on his shoulder. "You can undo this Buck I have faith in you. In us."

Daisy's scared voice rang out across the garden "My king she is gone he took her, Stormracer is gone!"

Walking over to stand beside her Buck kneeled down on one knee running a hand across the spot where the mare had been. Getting up he made his way back through the circle of guardsmen and townspeople only pausing long enough to tell Bane. "Send out word to every known soccer and sage by whatever means necessary tell them if they can find a way to undo this they can name their reward." Glancing back to the spot where Stormracer had been he added softly, "And send out word to every outlining village and town in the kingdom tell them what has happened but don't frighten them too much. They are going to have to be ready if worse comes to worse."

Bane gave Buck a questioning look, "Ready for what my king?"

Resuming his walk Buck muttered. "Ready to find a new home."

A hot dusty wind blew through the long line of heavily loaded wagons some still being loaded ruffling the mains and tails of horses and oxen yoked to them as people worked with ropes to secure their loads. The big courtyard was full with hundreds of riders from different lands who had come to help the stricken land. Among them a small group of riders gathered together talking, standing in the middle of them Domino listened to Lancer as he sit on a graying Carter the old horse pawing with impatience. "King Mulkies has said that his kingdom will take in as many of the people as they can so have all the rest. None of them can take all of the people but all of them will take some Brutus-hay kindness has not been forgotten the people will be well cared for."

Looking out the open gates of the city Domino watched as the dry wind blew huge dust devils across the dunes it had only been two weeks since the day that Stormracer had been brought down. Since that night the land had become unrecognizable. Only the Garden was untouched the rest of the kingdom had become a vast lifeless desert nothing any of the mages tried had reversed the curse. "And I am grateful for that." Domino told the man "As soon as the last of the wagons is ready you should go Shilo and I are going to try one more time to talk some sense into him hopefully all three of us will catch up to you before nightfall."

Looking at the empty castle Bane shook his head. "He still blames himself for this, I doubt you will get him to go with you. Truth to tell I am not sure it would be a good idea, word of what happened here and what he has become has traveled far. Not many people are going to feel comfortable with a cursed immortal living in their lands."

"He is not cursed and this was not his fault!" Shilo snapped at Bane "If our neighbors do not want him in their lands then we will find another place to live I will not leave him alone like this!"

"My apologies my lady," Bane replied embarrassed. "I was not implying otherwise."

Looking more uncomfortable by the second Bane added, "No one I know is blaming king Buck for this my lady the people all know he was under Molders influence the night that he cursed…The night Molder tricked him into trapping ... That he was not acting by his own.."

"Enough," Shilo snapped glaring at the tongue-tied man. "I know what you are trying to say and I thank you for the thought but maybe it would be best if you make sure that everyone is ready for the journey.

With à grateful nod of his head à obviously embarrassed Bane turned Cyclone and rode to the head of the waiting column. Watching him depart Domino put a comforting hand on Shilo's shoulder

"Don't be upset with him this is a hard time for everyone."

"Some more so than others," Shilo said softly looking at the towering throne room windows "Come on It will take both of us if we are going to talk any sense into him."

Without waiting for an answer she headed up the castle steps, following Domino paused long enough to look back over his shoulder at the long line of departing wagons and riders before turning and following her into the empty castle.

Chapter Seven
Friends of Old, Friends a New

Ashes woke with a start for a second he was not sure who or where he was. Sitting up he rubbed his blurry eyes trying to make sense of what had just happened. "Easy." A soft voice sounded close to him.

Blinking the fuzziness out of his eyes he looked up into Dominos concerned face "Those were your memories?" He ask.

Nodding Domino handed him a cup of cold water. "Not all of them just the ones that would give you an understanding of what has happened."

Shaking his head Ashes grumbled. "How long was I asleep?" Running a hand across the healed wounds on his side and leg, "It seemed like years, not the first time I had something like that happen though." Taking the cup gratefully Ashes lifted it to his lips draining it in quick gulps.

"True." Domino admitted. "But were before what you witnessed was the events of the present. What you have seen now where the events of long ago that brought about this great lands downfall. Your wounds and those of your horse were healed as you slept you both will need all your strength for what is to come"

"Yes." Ashes interrupted. "But I still don't know what it is that you think I can do about it, if the sorcerers in your time could not undo this I doubt that there is anything I could do."

"You are right, by yourself, there is nothing you can do," Domino told him. "But you are not going to be alone Buck and the Desert cats will be joining you on this journey. And as I told you before you will be reunited with friends and allies of before though they will not know you."

"Yea about that." Ashes said grudgingly. "No disrespect meant but how am I going to get these friends and allies who won't know me to help us? Can you at least give me an idea as to who they are?"

"You will know them," Domino said grinning. "When you see

them and at that time you will know what you must do to regain their trust. Have faith and all will be understood."

"I will do what I can to help but I still do not understand what it is you think I can do. Like I said before I am not a mage or sorcerer and I swore to give up the life as a mercenary. Although mayhap, in this case, that one can be overlooked."

Domino refilled Ashes empty cup. "You badly underestimate yourself. What is needed is not a mage or sorcerer but a good and brave man something you have proven yourself to be many times."

Ashes snorted. "I was a mercenary I fought for gold that does not make me a good or brave man."

"Truly?" Domino ask softly. "Tell me friend Ashes, if all you ever sought was gold, why so many times did you side with the weaker or poorer man? Why when the battle of Erton was over did you give your gold to the families who had lost their fathers and homes in the war? And in the Somopter feud when your forces were in retreat why did you risk everything to turn and ride back into the mist of the enemy to help a fallen man? Why when in the desert where you were given just one wish, did you not wish for a lifetime of power and wealth but instead wished for a world of peace where no man need fear war?"

Staring thoughtfully at his cup Ashes muttered. "I did what was right what I would hope any man would do."

"And that my friend is what makes you a good and brave man, even if you do not see yourself that way," Domino told him smiling.

"Huh" Ashes muttered draining the cup again. "Can you at least tell me more about what it is we are going and what we are going to do?"

"Molder has Stormracer trapped in crystal form using her power bit by bit to appease his master who in return grants him endless life," Domino explained. "But such is the power that she wields even trapped as she is now that he dare not try to take more than the smallest of slivers of her power at one time. He knows that if he did that her power would consume him and she would be free once more.

Even his master as powerful as he is cannot wield the power she possesses, not at one time. Molder is powerful and the dark one he worships a great deal more so but even combined their power is but a drop in the ocean compared to that Stormracer wields, a power so great that it can protect the gardens below us from the deserts touch trapped and weakened as she is. And her power is but a drop in the ocean of he who created all.

They know this and even though it angers them greatly they know that they must obey his laws. It is those laws that keep Molders' master at bay away from the world of men but once every hundred years under the dark sun Molders' master can for the briefest of moments come close enough to this world to impart his influence on those who will listen to his words. It is then that he takes for himself the power that Molder has stolen from Stormracer the smallest amount each tournament storing it away till his master returns for it. That is the reason he created the Frolla torment a very deadly race with a very tempting reward for the winner."

"I know about the Frolla tournament, almost every man does." Ashes said, "And only a fool would compete in it, one hundred men start the race and only one maybe two walk away whole some don't live to see the end of the race. And from what I understand Roxieca kings champion has won as long as anyone can remember. The only time the common man gets to even see the diamond trophy is when it is on display under heavy guard before the race."

"Yes," Domino agreed, "It is then when Molder draws the power from Stormracer, drawing on the unknowing crowds of greed and lust to aid him in doing so."

"So what we need to do is stop him before he can draw any of her power away when he is at his weakest." Ashes said thoughtfully "If we could find a way to kill him would that free her?"

"Regrettably it will not be as easy as that." Domino told him. "Molder is a very powerful mage and takes no chances defeating him in battle will be difficult, to say the least. And as long as he holds Stormracer captive drawing on her power to appease his master he is immortal and no weapon of mortal man can harm him."

Ashes grunted "So the first thing we need to do is find a way to break the curse and free Stormracer before we deal with Molder. Any ideas on how we can do that?"

"Several." A new voice sounded from the doorway, looking at the speaker Ashes was surprised to see the transformation Buck had made, from the tired and weary man who had rescued him from the Dark Arnka, to the proud king who had once ruled this land, "We can discuss them on the way to Roxieca, The horses are already saddled and our supplies are loaded we can leave as soon as you are ready."

The evening sun sat on the empty castle as the windswept desert sand quickly covered the strange tracks leaving the castle, two men, three horses and five Desert cats all traveling together to an uncertain fate.

It was just over a fortnight journey to Roxieca from the castle Ashes and Buck took turns both riding and leading the horses. Even though they spotted the Dark Arnka in the distance pacing them several times they had little fear of an attack with the Desert cats flanking them on both sides.

The two of them had spent most of the time debating on a plan that would have the best chance of success. They had two problems to deal with. First, .they needed to draw Molder and his guards away from Stormracer long enough for them to figure out how to free her. And second, how were they going to free her?

They were working out the last part of their plan when Ashes noticed that the landscape had started to change here and there trees and shrubs were starting to poke out of the sand. By midday the next day, their path was blocked by a dense forest covered with thick undergrowth and briers. Sitting back in his saddle Buck studied the forest stretching out as far as the eye could see on both sides of them. "If this is the Cupcake forest it has grown a lot since I last saw it, it used to only be a few leagues across."

Sliding out of his saddle Ashes tied the rains lose on a branch giving China room to graze as he checked for a path through the heavy brush. "Things change a lot in a thousand years old man." his voice muted by the leaves. "One thing is for sure we don't have time to go around not if we are going to make it to Roxieca in time for the tournament. If we can't find a trade road or game trail we will have to hack our way through."

A sudden movement from a briar patch on the edge of the woods caught Bucks attention turning in the saddle he brown blur shoot out of the forest and disappear in the thick brush of the glade. With Mulberry's white shape close behind watching the chase through the brush Buck recognized the Desert cats intended prey a Billdoc a small and very fast deer that could and was easily outrunning the bigger heavier Desert cat in the thick brush. "What happened?"

Ashes ask pushing his way back through the undergrowth to climb back onto Chinas back.

"Mulberry trying her luck with one of the local deer. She hasn't got a chance in hell of catching it throw. A shame really I could go for some fresh meat."

"Huh" Ashes grunted "If we were lucky she might save us a leg bone to chew on I've seen your friends eat remember? They don't leave much behind." pointing the way he had come Ashes muttered, "There is a game trail about a hundred feet in the woods not much but at least it is going in the right direction for now."

Nodding Buck let out a loud whooping call over his shoulder smiling when a broken roar sounded from the far side of the glade at Bucks questioning look he explained, "I know she can take care of herself and would find us when she was ready but sometimes she gets carried away and forgets she is not a cub anymore, I once had to track her ten leagues because she got lost playing with a leaf."

Almost on cue, Mulberry pushed through the brush looking embarrassed shaking twigs and leaves from her coat. Grinning at the big cat Ashes headed China into the woods "The trail is this way. If we are lucky maybe it goes all the way to the other side of the forest."

As luck would have it the trail split and changed course several times the men had to rely on their skill and trust their senses the dense trees making it hard to tell what direction they were going a darkening forest and the hidden roots that kept tripping the horses finely forced them to rest for the night.

Deciding that there was no danger of being spotted they light a small cooking fire and finished off the last of the fish that Buck had caught the day before. Sitting on a fallen tree branch Ashes twisted a long forked branch with blackened fish carcass over the fire after. Buck watched as Ashes pulled the stick back for the third time to blow out the burning lump that by now had little resemblance to a fish. "I would have thought that a mercenary would know how to cook his own food." The older man commented. "Eat a lot of cold meals do you?"

Picking at the blackened meat Ashes glared at his companion. "The meat is just as good one way or the other just a little darker is all."

"God must have a purpose for you," Buck laughed. "There is no other way you could have lived so long eating your own cooking, given the choice between your cooking and the stick I would sooner eat the stick"

"As you wish old man." Ashes grunted pulling the stick and the blackened fish back from the fire, "As soon as I finish with the fish the stick is all yours." Lying on the other side of the fire Cinnamon suddenly jerked her head up scenting the air a low growl rumbling deep in her throat. Moving quickly Buck jumped to his feet kicking dirt on the fire blanketing the clearing in darkness, dropping his meal Ashes rolled to his feet drawing his sword as he went.

Both man silently scanned the dark blackness of the surrounding woods trying to find what the Desert cats sensitive nose had sensed when a soft nicker sounded from the horses grazing in the brush. Heads held high the three horses were staring hard into the dark woods in the direction of a large grove of heavy brush in the distance.

As the two men surveyed the woods the silence was broken by a deep loud bray. Crouching down Ashes made his way toward the distant shelter of a dense brush as Buck hurried over to the calm the horses. Working his way thru the thick brush Ashes spotted something moving ghost-like through the trees on his left side.

Bringing his sword around, he stopped mid-turn as he recognized the lithe shape of Cactus Jack as she flanked her human companion through the woods. Looking on his other side he caught a quick glimpse of the other Desert cats pacing him. Hoping that the big cats would listen to him if necessary, he hurried through the woods.

 As he neared the darkened glade he heard the voices and saw the dark shapes of men on horseback moving through the underbrush. Looking around he was relieved to see the Desert cats crouching on their bellies watching him intently waiting for the signal to attack.

Good thing Buck had him work with the big cats every night getting them to follow his commands and it had surprised him how fast they had accepted him. They were very intelligent, learning quickly he was grateful for that now. And as long as they were downwind of the stranger's horses he hoped they would stay hidden.

But as it turned out the wind had other ideas just as the newcomers were getting close enough for him to make out their words the wind shifted carrying the strong scent of predators to several horses' sensitive nostrils.

With a loud snort, the lead horse stopped dead in its tracks blowing hard starting in Ashes direction along with over half dozen mounted men.

"Damn," Ashes whispered thinking quickly he realized that there was little chance of him and the Desert cats slipping away without being detected. Taking a chance that the strangers would not react hostel he stepped out of the brush into plain sight. Signaling to the Desert cats to stay put and praying that they would not misunderstand the signal. Holding his hands in plain sight he walked casually toward the heavily armed group.

"Easy strangers." He called out knowing that Buck was hidden in the darkness watching and listening. Stopping halfway between them and the Desert cats he watched the group closely for any signs of hostility ready to dive back into the heavy underbrush if necessary.

Nudging his horses closer the lead rider studied Ashes suspiciously "You want to tell us what a man would be doing wandering around on foot this deep in the woods this late at night?"

Ashes could only stare in disbelief as the man finished speaking even in the darkest woods there was no doubting who the speaker was. Taking a step closer to be sure he barely stopped himself from running forward to greet the big man who in another place had been the commander of his armies, Fredrex.

As the big man watched him impatiently waiting for an answer a second rider road beside him on a squat long-eared mount. At first, Ashes thought that the donkey was holding one ear tilted back but a closer look showed the right ear missing just above the skull.

Scanning the darkened woods with piercing blue eyes she muttered: "I don't trust this Fredrex he is not alone there is someone else out there Brian hears them." Drawing her dagger the women glared at Ashes.

"Tell your friends to come out into the open or I swear I will spill your guts all over the forest!" looking past her Ashes saw the other members of the party readying for an attack spacing themselves out watching the dark woods warily swords drawn.

Fredrex put a restraining hand on Abby's wrist. "Relax women." He told her softly. " I know there are more out there but let's give this one a chance to explain before you go gutting him, only a fool fights a battle he does not have to."

Still glaring Abby nodded at Ashes. "You heard him start talking, and if this is a trick or ambush you won't live to see your friends fail."

Recovering from his surprise Ashes jerked a thumb over his shoulder at the heavy brush behind him. "It is not a trick, and I never said I was alone." He told them in a friendly voice. "My friends are out there close waiting to see what happens there is no telling how strangers are going to greet travelers in a strange woods especially late at night. Best not to take chances as you said only a fool fights a needless battle."

"So they decided to sacrifice you, did they?" Abby asked wolfishly "Sounds like the kind of friends you could do without."

"Coming out to meet you was my idea, I have no desire to see you or your friends lose your lives for no reason." Ashes told her truthfully." And as far as my friends go, I don't think my life is the one in danger, Stand fast and make no threatening moves and you won't be harmed," Ashes said slapping his leg loudly three times in a rapid session.

As Ashes slapped his leg both Fredrex and Abby tensed watching the woods readying their swords for battle stopping suddenly as five large shapes melted out of the shadows surrounding the riders and their nervous mounts.

"Don't be foolish." a new voice sounded out of the darkness. "Like my young friend said we have no desire to see any of you lose your lives, but whether you live or die right now depends on you. Make a foolish move and I promise you it will be your last." Running a hand along Banes side as he walked past him Buck stepped out into the open his green eyes glowing softly in the darkness.

Ashes looked around taking in the rest of the newcomers and the Desert cats in one glance trusting Buck to keep an eye on the lead two riders. A feeling of disbelief growing as he looked from face to face, seeing friends he thought never to see again. Clip, Diego, Vale, Thunk, Notie. And standing back to back a small silvered haired young women and a short stout young man who were watching the Desert cats with a look of both fear and wonder, Snowflake, and Blueberry.

Looking at them he could hear Dominos voice again in his head "You will not be alone you will be reunited with friends of the past friends you know but who have not yet met you."

He had told Buck the story of Zlarora and what had happened but Buck would have no idea what his companions in that kingdom looked like and none of the newcomers would even know of the strange land or what roles they had played there. In that other place he knew these people and what to expect from them he had trusted them with his life. And he was willing to bet that they were the same in this world as the other, still good people he had to act fast and tread carefully. For the moment everything was quiet but a foolish move could change that very quickly.

Too many times in his life he had seen situations like this go bad Abby was already glaring at Buck with undisguised hate in her eyes. "Sorcerer!" The women hissed between clenched teeth. The air was filled with a growing tension that had the Desert cats pacing back and forth if any of his onetime friends made an aggressive move he was not sure that they would be able to stop the big cats in time.

Deciding to take a risk Ashes turned and started walking back in the direction of their camp calling back at the bewildered group. "We made camp just over the rise you are welcome to join us if you want and we can talk this over. Or you can try your luck with the Desert cats, word of warning though their last real meal was two days ago they're proudly getting pretty hungry about now." Without waiting for an answer he pushed his way thru the brush back to the glowing embers of the fire.

Staring at Ashes disappearing form Buck shrugged and started to follow his companion, giving the strangers a departing glare the Desert cats turned and followed their human friends into the darkness.

After watching them for a second, Fredrex waved to the rest of the party. "What the hell." He growled. "Come on, they're either honest or insane let's go find out which one it is and at any rate I am not sure I want to be traveling these woods at night not knowing were those damn cats are."

Following Ashes and Buck Fredrex and the rest of their party walked into the camp just as Ashes was putting more wood on the fire blowing on the embers till the dry branches burst into flame. Sitting on the other side of the fire Buck Called to their guest nodding at the fire and the rest of the uneaten fish. "There is food if you are hungry we already ate but you are more than welcome to what is left if you want it."

Looking around for the Desert cats Fredrex spotted them lying scattered just outside of the firelight around the camp. "We appreciate the offer, but we have a long-standing rule about knowing who we are sharing our meals with. We have of yet to decide if you are friend or foe."

Sitting back Buck stretched out his arms with a yawn. "If we had any ill intent you would have known it by know." He said looking at the big cats. "We are just travelers on our way to Roxieca for the tournament, we had just made camp for the night when we heard your donkey and wanted to find out who else would be stumbling thru this damn forest this late at night."

Leading Topper, Clip was The last of the group to make his way through the underbrush pulling a briar vine off his shirt he gave Brian an annoyed glare. "Can't say as how that surprises me this group could not sneak up on an army of deaf man with that donkey braying every five feet."

Standing next to Brian Abby gave the donkey's ear a fond scratch "Don't pay that fool any mind Brian" She said gently. "At least when you bray it is for a good reason unlike some who spend most of their lives spouting drivel or whining. You know little brother if you don't like his braying you are free to leave." She added glaring at Clip over the donkey's back.

Little brother? Ashes thought that was different in Zalora, Abby and Clip were not siblings at least he did not think they were the thought had never occurred to him but the two did have a lot in common both were very proud and strong-willed and both were very good at what they did. Surprised he looked hard at the two, Damn even in the dim firelight there was no denying the strong resemblance. In Zalora he had never seen them together. "Well that explains a lot" Ashes muttered louder than he intended.

Standing just the other side of the fire from him Vale gave him a questioning look "What explains a lot?" The older man ask.

Thinking quick Ashes pointed over Vales shoulder at the night sky were several stars could be seen through a gap in treetops. "Like I said before we were making our way to Roxieca when we started into this damn dense forest. And I lost my compass several weeks back so we have been traveling by the sun and stars you can't see either in this place or not till just now anyway." Looking at Buck Ashes hoped the man would catch on. "We drifted south quite a bit we're going to have to pick up the pace if we want to get to Roxieca in time for the tournament."

"You keep saying you are going to the tournament," Fredrex said, "To watch or are you planning on running in the race?"

Reaching over Buck picked up his water jug untying the opening to take a drink "My young friend here has a pretty impressive horse that he seems to think has a good chance of taking the prize." he told them.

"Really," Fredrex snorted. Looking around at the trees surrounding the camp "I have seen a lot of impressive horses run that race and so far none have beaten the champions mount, where is this horse?"

Getting to his feet Ashes let out a short sharp whistle that was answered by the sound of branches breaking and heavy hoofs steps as the big stallion shoved his way through the underbrush trotting over to stand next to Ashes. "Damn," Vale whispered "That is one hell of a stallion, the only other horses I have seen that size are the heavy horses that pull the wagons in the Quacker forest but they are shorter of leg than him. What is his breeding?"

Scratching Chinas withers Ashes shook his head "I bought him from a Traveler years ago when he was a colt, he was sickly at the time and the man just wanted to be rid of him never said anything about who his sire or dam was or how he came by him."

"Not sickly now." Vale muttered appreciatively "That is the strongest looking horse I have ever seen, been in a fight or two I take it." He added nodding at a scar running the length of China's side.

"One or two." Ashes agreed.

Sliding Toppers saddle off, Clip glanced at the big stallion. "A horse like that would bring a high price in any market just as a breeding stud, seems strange that you would risk him in a battle when you could rent him out as a stud. I am betting a lot of people would pay well for a colt from his line. I know a man in Roxiecas high court that would pay you his weight in gold for him if you wanted to sell him."

"We have had our arguments over the years but I would not give him up for any price." Ashes told the slim man.

"But you would throw away his life for a chance to win a diamond trophy that will never be yours!" Abby snapped. "Do your horse and yourself a favor and go back to where you came from you have no chance of winning that race. Even with a sorcerers help." She added glaring at Buck.

"That is twice tonight that you have called me a sorcerer young lady," Buck said softly watching the sparks from the fire as he stirred it with a stick. Looking up his eyes glowed with a light other than that from the fire. "I can see where you might mistake me for one but you would be wrong. I have nor do I wish to weld any magic abilities of any kind. Whether you chose to believe that or not is up to you I have no control over that."

Still glaring Abby softened her tone "Say what you will but I have only seen one other man with eyes like yours and He almost killed me. Why should I trust you?"

"Because he is telling the truth, Abby" Snowflake said softly as she stepped from behind the bigger women. The fire light set her long silver-white hair aglow as she stopped in front of Buck staring into the man's eyes. "I sense power in him, very old, very great power but not magic or sorcery." Closing her eyes she reached a hand out till it was almost touching his face. "Something older and far more powerful." Half turning she stared at Ashes with a piercing gaze. 'There is something about this one as well, it is not so now but at one time he was touched by a great power. I sense no evil in either of them."

"Huh" Fredrex grunted looking back and forth from one man to the other. "Meet Snowflake we found her and her brother Blueberry lost and starving in the high mountains last year. And in case you have not guessed, she can sense sorcery or witchcraft and the like." Nodding at the smallest of the man in the group. "And Blueberry there is the best healer I have ever seen gets along with animals too, can tell what they are thinking or something like that"

"Feeling not thinking," Blueberry muttered. "It is not the same thing."

"Well in any case." Vale told them "Snowflake here seems to trust you so I guess we will as well. At least till you give us a reason not to."

"Yea fine." Abby snapped. "We're all friends now that still does not change the fact that you have no chance of winning the tournament all you are going to do is get your horse and yourself killed if you run in it."

"You seem pretty sure about that." Ashes said, "What makes you so certain we will lose?"

"Because you are racing against a demon!" Abby yelled, "I know, we ran in that race and I damn near lost Brian because of it!"

Notie spoke from the shadows. "The torment is the reason we came to this place to begin with. We heard about the diamond trophy and thought we had had the perfect plan for winning. And we did, there should have been no way we could have lost."

Looking at Buck and Ashes he explained. "The terrain in the race varies wildly from one place to the next making it hard for any one horse to keep a lead." Pointing at a small appaloosa mare he went on. "Topper there is Clips horse and in tight turns and short burst she has no equal Clip is just there for the look of things." He added with a grin, nodding at a wild-eyed long-legged brown mare "Babe is Thunk's mount and once she gets going nothing can run her down or catch her." Looking at a glaring Abby rubbing the donkey's ear he finished. "And over rough and dangerous ground Brian is untouchable the damn Donkey is a half mountain goat. We thought that with those three working as a team in the race would be sure to win."

"We were winning!" Abby blurted out. "We were in the mountains in the last league of the race Brian had the lead by over a mile, He was winning! If it had been a fair race he would have won!"

Standing up Buck walked over to give the donkey a soft pat on the neck. "What happened?" He ask the glowering women.

"Like I said we were in the lead." Abby continued. "Topper and Babe couldn't keep up on the rough ground so Clip and Thunk fell back to watch my backside for an ambush, that seems to happen a lot to the leaders in the tournament. We were coming out of the last canyon about two miles from the city and the road was clear there was nothing between us and finish line. When the road in front of us burst into fire, I mean the rocks on the ground melted!" She said in disbelief. "I never saw anything like that before, I did not know what was going on. Till Molder came riding that thing out of the fire and looked at me all smug and confident "A women", He said, "The closest anyone has come to winning and it is a women it is almost a shame to kill you."

"Then that demon he was riding attacked. It hit Brian broadside before we knew it had moved nothing mortal moves that fast. I was knocked off, I saw Brian fighting with that thing and was going to help him but before I could get back to my feet Molder hit me knocked me near senseless and started trying to tear my clothes off."

Abby ran a loving hand over Brian's nose. "Brian saw what was happening he turned his back on that demon to help me, he let Molder have it with both hind hooves knocked that filth off me and saved my life, but it cost him. Molders mount laid his back leg open to the bone and bit off his ear. I was half senseless but I swore to myself that I would die before I let that thing touch me again or hurt Brian anymore. I found my sword and got back to my feet but both of them were gone by then."

"I think he knew that Clip and Thunk were close and decided that I was not worth the trouble so he just left." Pausing Abby stroked Brian's muzzle thoughtfully before turning to Ashes with a meaningful look. "So you can see I have some insight about what I am talking about, if you care for your horse at all you will forget about that damn race and go back to where you came from."

For a second Ashes was unsure what to say he wanted to tell this proud woman he was sorry for what had happened to her and Brian but he knew her too well. She was not asking for nor would she want his sympathy. After debating with himself he decided that for better or worse to tell these people the reason that they journeyed here.

Looking over at Buck he saw the older man nod in agreement. Glancing around the camp Ashes cursed softly under his breath well he thought I guess I am about to find out how much like your other selves you really are. "If the only reason we were here was for the trophy then I might take your advice." He told Abby, "But we are here for another reason one in which we need your help. Tell me how much do any of you know about the kingdom of Brutus-hay and the legend of Stormracer?"

Chapter Eight
To Free a Legend

"**S**tormracer and Brutus- hay?!" Notie laughed. "Only what I have heard in the stories that old man spin in the taverns. But what does a child's bedtime story have to do with any of this?"

"Far more than you know young- man," Buck told him. "That child's bedtime story is what will decide the fate of this land and in time all the lands of this world."

Still standing next to Abby he put a comforting hand gently on her shoulder guiding her towards the fire. "Come, sit, all of you. You told us your story allow us to tell you one in return, and when we are done you can decide for yourselves if we are insane or not and if you will help us or go on your way. Either way, we must do what we came here to do, listen now and you will understand why. First, allow me to tell you something about myself, my parents are lord Dragon and the lady Shay once king and queen of the great land of Brutus-hay and I am Buck the last king to sit on the throne and the man who brought down the curse that destroyed that kingdom."

In the shocked silence that followed Buck and Ashes took turns telling their disbelieving audience their stories. At first, they were met with questions full of doubt and sarcasm that began to fade as the night wore on. By morning the question was not if Ashes and Buck were telling the truth but how could they stop Molder and free Stormracer? Several plans were discussed and debated until finally, they settled on the one that everyone agreed had the best chance of succeeding.

As was with their first plan Ashes and China would enter the tournament, everyone agreed that Ashes and the big stallion would have the best chance if it came down to a fight with Molder and his demon mount as had happened with Abby and Brian. The rest of the group along with the Desert cats would use the race as a distraction to try to break into the heavily guarded room where Stormracer was being kept and free her from her diamond prison. How they were going to free her was something that they hoped to work out by the time they got to Roxieca.

Vale looked through the treetops at the early morning sky. The sun had not yet risen and one or two stars still be seen. "Well, I don't know about the rest of you but I could use some food and sleep I fight demons best on a full stomach."

Rubbing his eyes with a hand Lancer yawned. "I could use some food and sleep myself, but do we have time? The race starts in three days and it will take almost that long to get there."

"We can eat and rest till high sun I know narrow pass through the Patches mountains that will be easier on the horses and save us a day's travel, "Fredrex told them. "I doubt that there is anyone else in these woods."

"Grinning he jerked a thumb at the slumbering shapes of the Desert cats scattered around the camp. "And even if there is they would be fools to try anything with our big friends there. So everyone eat something and try to get some sleep, I have a feeling we are all going to need as much as we can get."

Having traveled the day before and staying up all night no one in the party argued with the big man everyone was tired after making sure that the horses were cared for and a quick meal they were all grateful to get some sleep even if it was only a few hours

. Buck woke first the bright sun shining through the treetops blinding him. Confused it took him a minute to recall the events of the night before, getting to his feet he woke the others. Seeing the same dumbfounded look in their faces he felt a little less foolish. Once everyone was awake it only took a few minutes to break camp and head out. And with Fredrex leading the way they found the pass with no problem saving them even more time than they thought. Sunset two days later saw them riding out of the last foothills and into the grassy plains stretching out before the crowded city of Roxieca.

Riding at a fast trot they stuck to the brushy plains and avoided the main roads trying not to draw any attention to their party. With the tournament getting ready to start a large party of strangers would not likely draw much more than a quick glance from a passing city patrol. But throw in five large predators and there were going to be questions.

Just before they ran out of cover Ashes lead the group into a ravine to go over the plan one last time turning China to face the others. "Alright, this is where we split up China and I will take the main road and enter in the race. Are you sure you heard right about what the entry fee was?" He ask Notie

Nodding his head Notie tossed a bag of coins at Ashes. "The fee goes up every race, greedy bastards! But from what I overheard in the last tavern we were in, that should be enough to cover the fee. With a few coins left for you to find a place for you and the stallion to get a meal and some rest your both going to need it."

Catching the bag with one hand Ashes tied it to his belt. "We missed the displaying of the trophy but that should not matter as far as you being able to enter in the race," Fredrex told him. "The race starts at sunrise, we will make camp here for the night, and we will be able to see the riders in the race leave the city. When that happens we will sneak in as best we can." He added with a meaningful look at the pacing Desert cats. "Make our way to the vault room and if everything goes as planned free Stormracer. Do you have any idea how we are going to do that yet?" He ask Buck

"Not for sure." Buck admitted "But I have an idea."

"An idea?" Abby snapped. "With all due respect old king I hope that by the time we get into the vault room you have somewhat more than an idea."

"Abby!" Blueberry said reproachfully. "We all are risking our lives for this none more so than any other this is not the time for sarcasm."

Glaring at the little man Abby opened her mouth to reply when Snowflake cut her off. "I don't know if it helps but my mother used to always sing me a song when we had really bad storms and I was scared and couldn't sleep. I was just a child and I don't remember all of it but there was one verse I never forgot." Closing her eyes the small woman lifted her head singing softly. "In a time of uncertainty and a time of dark the shadows carried her away, and when man accepts the truth and finally understands, in a storm's fury god will return her to us to one day." Looking embarrassed Snowflake fell silent.

'Huh," Fredrex muttered, "Does that make any sense to you friend Buck?"

Whispering the words to himself Buck suddenly reached into his shirt pulling out a golden chain with a shimmering medallion twisting on it. "In a storm's fury." He said thoughtfully. "She said that the power of the hurricane was within this medallion. That I would one day need it."

Staring at the slowly turning medallion he cursed softly. "All this time the answer was right in front of me, all these years."

"Maybe" Ashes put in quickly. "But I don't think that is all there is to it Both Stormracer and Domino told me that all the pieces had to be in place to free her, meaning all of us." He said waving his arm to take in the surrounding group of humans and animals. "The amulet may have a part to play in this but not by itself. Have faith old man you have not got senile yet, it will come to you." He laughed reassuringly. "You try to get some sleep and trust that when the time comes we will know what needs to be done"

"He's right." Diego Agreed "I don't know much about cures or magic and such but I am betting that it takes more than a strong wind to break one."

"And at any rate," Abby said thoughtfully. "If that thing really holds the power of a hurricane it may not be a good idea to use it without knowing for sure, best to use it as a last resort."

Nodding in agreement Buck slipped the chain back into his shirt. "Good point. She did say that once I release it I would only be able to control it for a short time. You better get to the city you need to enter the race and find a place for you and China to get some rest." Looking around at the others. "The rest of you better get some sleep, I will keep watch and try to figure out what we are going to do when the time comes."

Giving the reins a gentle tug Ashes headed China toward the red twinkling lights of the city. " We have been racking our brains for a fortnight trying to decide what we are going to do, maybe that's the problem, why don't all of you try to get some sleep and trust that when the time comes we will know what needs to be done. Have faith old man you have not got senile yet, it will come to you." He laughed reassuringly

Ashes and China made their way to the city at an easy trot after weeks of travel and all the stories he had heard of the city he was more than a little disappointed when he saw it for the first time. It was a big city but not the biggest city he had ever seen or the most impressive it was one of the most heavily guarded though. As he rode through the main gates he counted no less than twenty guards standing watch and twice as many manning the walls.

The tournament and the displaying of the trophy was probably the reason for the heavy guard. It was his hope that once it started the race would provide the distraction his friends would need to find and free Stormracer. Just as he started to pass the last of the guards a man stepped out of a hidden alcove by the gate to stand in front of China blocking his path.

Reining the stallion to a stop he noticed the rest of the guards moving in to form a circle around him. Sitting back in the saddle Ashes tried to look relaxed after all there was no way these men could know what his friends and he were planning, was there? Giving a friendly smile he told the thin man. "Came a long way to run in your race ran into some trouble in the mountains that slowed me down a day or two I am not too late to enter am I?"

Shaking his head the man pointed through the gates to a large building with lamps still burning in several windows. "The magistrate will be taking entries till midnight going to be a big race this year so far over fifty riders have entered."

"Not that any of them have a chance." The guard next to him commented. "I have seen five tournaments in my life and the royal family has won every one. And as long as they keep the breeding pure I don't see anyone beating them. I don't know if you have seen the horse you will be racing against stranger I have, and it is the strongest horse I have ever seen. Though yours would be a close second." He added giving China an appreciative look. "Who knows maybe if you're careful and lucks with you-you might win. My money is still on the king. No offense."

You might change your mind if you knew what I knew Ashes thought. Thanking the guards he headed into the city stopping in front of the building that the guards pointed out. Sliding out of the saddle he let the reins hang loose on the neck of the stud so he could graze on the grass next to the building. Knowing the horse well he knew that there was no way the stud would wander off and he pitied the man who was fool enough to try to steal him

As he was heading for the doorway to the building he heard a soft nicker from the shadows. Looking around he spotted a steel dust mare with a worn saddle and bridle tied to a tree just the other side of China a fact that did not escape the stallions notice. Turning around Ashes caught up the studs rains tying them to a tree out of sight of the mare. "Mind your manners. You're going to need your strength for the race," He snapped at the stallion. Heading back into the building he had no trouble finding the magistrate's office being the only room in the large building with a lamp burning made it easy to find.

He heard the voices even before he was halfway to the room "Eight gold pieces? But that

Is almost twice what the fee was for the last race." A young voice sounded Stopping in the doorway he saw a young man barely in his teens standing in front of a large table with a stout older man sitting behind it.

Looking genuinely sorry the older man replied. "I am not the one who sets the fee son I collect the gold and enter you in the race. I wish I could help you but I have to follow the rules like everyone else. If you need I will wait an extra hour before closing the register to give you time to make up what you are short."

Looking defeated the young man muttered "No. It would not matter I sold everything I had to get what coin I have, I have nothing left."

"Why do you want to enter in this race boy?" Ashes ask entering the room. "This is not a game, men get killed running in this race."

"I know that!" The young man said glowering at Ashes. "My father and brother both died in this race last time, they never even got close to the finish I am going to race and I am going to finish for both of them I don't care about the trophy."

"And what of your mother after losing her husband and one of her sons who would that leave to care for her if she would lose you as well?" Ashes ask Looking at the boy. There was something strangely familiar about this boy he could not help the feeling he had seen this boy before but were?

Dropping his eyes the young man muttered "I have no mother she died when I was born I am the last in my family line."

"And if you were to die in this race like your father and brother your line will come to an end." The nearest guard said. "Maybe son you would be wiser to use what coin you have to find a home and a wife."

"I swore on my fathers and brothers grave that I would finish this race for them and I will." The young man snapped looking from the guard to Ashes. "Kena is a strong, fast horse I know she can finish the race if I can get the gold I need." Some of the defiance melted out of the young man "I just don't know where to get it."

Sighing Ashes ask the man behind the table. "How much is he short?"

"Two gold pieces." the stout man replied looking at the pile of coins in front of him

Untying the bag from his belt Ashes dumped the contents onto the table counting the coins with a finger "It is eight gold pieces to enter right?" he ask the man behind the table.

"Yes," the man replied. "And if I am counting right you have nine, enough for you but that still is one coin short of what you need if you mean to help this young man enter."

Before Ashes could reply the guard that had spoken before flipped a coin onto the table with a grin "I did well with the dice last night consider this an investment boy. I bet a few coins on you to finish and if you do, I make back everything I bet, and more. If you get killed you remember me in the afterlife and vouch for me I will probably need all the help I can get."

The young man gave both Ashes and the guard a grateful look "Thank you both of you if it was anything else I would not take your charity but I promise you that if I win I will pay you back a hundredfold and even if I don't win I will repay you somehow."

Giving the young man a friendly slap on the back Ashes laughed, "Just live through the race and I will consider the debt repaid"

Grinning the guard nodded his head "The same goes for me boy but if you by some chance win. I won't turn down the hundred gold prices"

"All right," the squat man said "All I need is your horse name and your own"

"My horse is Kenya and my name is Zephyr," the young man said.

At the man's questioning look Ashes spoke up. "Ashes, and my horses name is China".

" Very well ." The man said " That is Ashes riding China and Zepher riding Kena." He noted writing down their names "The race starts when the sunlight hits the crystal tower." At Ashes questioning look he handed the two a slip of paper "Don't worry stranger when it happens you will know, do yourself a favor and don't be looking at the crystal when it happens more than one man has been blinded that way. Here are your verification forms don't lose them you will need them to get past the guards at the entrance to the stables." Taking the offered slip of paper Ashes thanked the man and left the room.

As Ashes was gathering up China's reins Zephyr called to him "I have a stall a friend let me use for Kenya there is plenty of room for both horses if you think the stud will behave, Kena's season is not for a while yet. I was planning on bedding down in the barn for the night myself you and China are welcome if you have nowhere else to go."

Swinging up in the saddle Ashes nodded at the young man, "Lead the way, I am warning you though China snores"

Buck rolled out his bedroll next to the slumbering Cinnamon. Patting the big cat on the side as he stretched out resting his head on her flank. "They must really like you." Diego commented.

Grunting Buck closed his eyes. "This old girl and I have known each other a long time we get along pretty well, a few spats now and then but nothing major."

"You're still in one piece so it must not be" Thunk laughed, looking thoughtfully at Buck he ask. "You been around a long time right?"

"That's what I just said" Buck muttered sleepily "why?"

Still looking thoughtful Thunk rubbed the side of his face with a hand. "Have you ever heard of the fire rose?" He asked.

Laying out her own bedroll on the other side of the camp Abby growled "Thunk for god's sake will you let it drop? It is a child's story nothing more I swear if you bring it up one more time I will scream!"

Walking into the camp from checking the horse's Clip laughed. "And how would that be any different from every other day sister?"

"Because little brother this time I will be doing it as I am standing on your headless body," Abby muttered glaring at her sibling

"The trouble with you two is that your exactly alike, both stubborn, loud and proud, how the two of you have lived this long and not gutted each other is something I will never figure out." Fredrex growled "We are all going to need our strength in the morning if we are going to be awake and ready as soon as the race starts. So everyone gets some sleep, as close as we are to the city we better post a guard. I am not tired so I will keep a look out if I get tired I will wake someone."

Mutters of agreement came from around the camp as everyone settled in for the night. Lifting his head off Cinnamons warm side Buck squinted through the light of the small fire at Thunk. "To answer your question, yes I have heard of the Fire rose but only in tails carried in from far off lands it is a legend almost as old as Stormracer's herself. But Aside from the stories I know nothing about it."

Nodding at the older man Thunk sighed "That is alright, I just thought that maybe being somewhat older you might know more about it than what the stories tell, thanks anyway."

Finding a log to sit on Fredrex kept a vigilant watch on the empty fields and road leading to the dark city as the rest of the camp slept. Even though they proudly did not believe him what he had told his friends was true. He was not tired or sleepy, he was worried for his friends, in the morning they were going to ride into a crowded city, try to sneak in a heavily guarded room and possibly fight a sorcerer of great power to free a creature of legend and try not to get killed doing it. Lifting his head he stared into the sky. "I have not ask you for much god, but I am asking you now please keep my friends safe tomorrow." Sighing he shifted his weight on the log and stared at the city lost in thought.

Chapter Nine
Race for a Legend

A tug on his arm woke Ashes, opening his eyes he could barely make out the outline of China pulling his head back over the stall door in the early morning light. Nickering the stallion pawed impatiently at the hard ground a loud banging echoing in the stables as his hoof struck the stall door. Sitting up Ashes rubbed his eyes as he got to his feet looking around for the bag of grain that Zephyr had bartered the stable owner out of the night before. "Give me a minute to find it you hog in horsehide!" Ashes snapped "You are not going to starve to death any time soon." Finding the bag in the darkness he untied it and half-filled a feed Bucket carrying it into the stall he divided it up between the two horses.

"I have some dried meat and hardtack if you are hungry." A groggy voice said from behind him. Looking over his shoulder he saw Zephyr blinking away the last sleep from his eyes.

"Starving." Ashes told the young man truthfully "I doubt we are going to get much chance to eat once the race starts."

Pulling open his saddlebags Zephyr dug out the dried rations breaking them in half and handing Ashes his share. "You're not here just for the race are you?" He ask around a mouth full of meat. "The other racers all have the same look in their eyes like my father and brother had. You don't" He added softly staring hard at Ashes in the dim light.

Swallowing a mouth full of dried bread Ashes Muttered. "I could give a damn about winning the race son but I will help you finish as much as I can. Just stick close to me and when I tell you, ride like hell for the finish and don't look back."

"If you are not here for the race then why…?" Zepher started to ask before Ashes cut him off.

"There is not the time to explain and you would not believe me anyway, just trust me boy and do as I tell you and maybe we both might live to see tomorrow. Now get a move on we don't want to miss the start of the race." Grabbing a brush Ashes started grooming China and checking him over in the dim light making sure he was ready for the race.

The last stars were still out as the two roads through the city but the streets were already crowded with people hurrying not to miss the race. The crowd thinned out as they approached the heavily guarded street at the edge of the city where the race would start. After taking their entry slips the guards stepped aside to let them pass. "Best you should hurry your almost too late strangers." The closest Guard said. "The sun will hit the crystal any minute now. You two are the last to arrive so you will have to start in the rear flank."

Looking at the rapidly growing light on the skyline Ashes saw the man was right the race was only minutes away from starting. Nudging China with a boot he guided the big horse to join the other riders in the race. Glancing around to make sure that Zephyr and Kena were still with him he spotted a familiar form trotting a huge horse through the crowd of racers making his way to the front of the group, Molder.

Shoulder length red hair blew behind him as he trotted past Ashes but aside from that, the man looked just as Ashes had last seen him in Dominos memories. Ashes felt slightly foolish when he caught his self-ducking his head as the man passed, there was no way Molder would know him. Watching the man ride to lead Ashes understood what Abby had been talking about. The horse Molder road was unlike any he had ever seen. A stallion huge and heavy muscled his body was riddled with scars from both cuts and burns with a short cropped black mane and tail he had either been born with no ears or they had been cut or bitten off. But the strangest thing was his color. In all his life Ashes had never seen a horse marked like him. From tail to withers he was a dark blood brown, his neck was yellowish white bleeding into his jet black head outlining cold deep set pure white eyes. Abby had called him a demon looking at him now Ashes agreed China and him were literally in a ride for their lives.

The sudden flash from the crystal as the sun's rays hit it caught Ashes off guard, cursing at himself for getting distracted he let the rains go slack as China leaped forward along with a hundred other horses and riders. The race had started...

Fredrex had let the other sleep waking them early so everyone would be fully awake and ready when the race started. Being the first to be ready Clip watched the riders charge out the city gate from Toppers back. "Looks like the race has started!" He called back to the others.

Swinging into his saddle Bluesky trotted his pony Hopper stopping next to Topper. "Can you see who is winning?" He ask squinting in the distance.

"All I see is a herd of horses and dust." Clip told him. "And anyway it makes no difference who is in the lead right now in this kind of race the start of the race is all for a show."

"True," Abby said coming up on Clips another side. "Once they are outside the city gates most of these riders will not even see each other again till the end of the race if they live that long that is."

"Well, that is not our concern," Notie Said riding up from behind. ' The race is Ashes worry all we have to do is ride into the city with a pack of Desert cats and ask them to kindly let us take their most prized possession, easy."

"We all know what is at stake there is no use sitting here complaining about it," Vale told him. Nodding at the Desert cats he ask Buck "Have you figured out how we are going to get our friends here past the guards?"

"I have been watching the city all night," Fredrex said before Buck could answer. "And the main gates are pretty well guarded, but there is a side door hidden just below the north corner torrent. I think it leads to the barracks. Some cities have doors like that to sneak supplies and the like in without being spotted if they are ever under siege. I saw a couple of guards going in and out with torches just before midnight."

"I bet that with the race going on those barracks will be empty and there is no one on the north wall right now so I doubt that anyone will be watching the door. Buck you take Blueberry and Snowflake with you along with the Desert cats head for the door and wait. I will take the others through the main gate we will open the door from the inside. If I remember right the barracks are right next to the main castle and the vault room. If we are lucky we might get that far without being spotted. Any questions?" He ask.

"Hundreds" Diego muttered sourly. "But I don't think I would like the answers so let's do this."

Having no way to get a full-grown horse threw the man-size doorway Buck and his party had to leave their mounts with Fredrex and the others. At first, there was some worry about if they could make it to the castle on foot fast enough to meet the others when the door was opened.

Even if the barracks were empty they there was no telling how long it would remain that way and every minute they were there increased the danger of them getting caught. Bucks answer to the problem surprised everyone putting a hand on Sugar britches shoulder he climbed onto his back tucking his feet behind the big cat's front legs. Smiling at the other two he nodded at Cinnamon and Cactus Jack. "Go ahead" He told them "I have ridden them several times it is just like a horse but with a longer gait."

Looking unsure but exited Blueberry pulled himself up on Cinnamon with Snowflake following suite on Cactus Jack. Letting out a childlike laugh as the big cat stepped off forcing her to grab a hand full of soft fur to keep her balance. "Dam" Abby muttered to Clip "I am almost jealous." Splitting up the two parties headed for their destinations.

As Fredrex had hoped with most everyone distracted by the race there were few guards keeping watch, both groups made it to the door without any trouble. Pulling the heavy door open Fredrex was greeted by a disgusted Buck. "A drunken blind man could keep a better look out than these fools, for God's sake how do you miss someone riding up to your city on a Desert cat?"

"Don't bemoan it old king. "Fredrex laughed "Just pray that our luck holds out, I will be happy if we make it to the end of the day without losing any limbs."

The day of the tournament was a day of celebration for the city in which the race was only part. Once the riders left the city gates the only way for the spectators to know what was happening was from the reports relayed in by the spotters stationed around the race path. So once the racers left the city gates the streets filled with people in a day-long celebration.

This worked out well for Buck and the others even with the Desert cats in tow they were able to make their way unseen to the main castle. Trying to stay hidden in the shadows of a dark hallway Fredrex watched the guards in front of the big doors. "I count six guarding the doors probably more inside" he muttered thoughtfully.

"No way to sneak up on them either," Notie said standing beside the big man. "And no way to get close to them without being seen that I can see, you have any ideas?" He ask Buck.

"I do" Abby grunted, unbuckling her sword belt she handed it to Clip along with her daggers. Still talking she unbuttoned her vest and shirt taking off her shirt before buttoning the vest back up. "The celebration is going on and the city is full of people right now a lot of them from other cities. So it is a pretty good bet that not everyone knows their way around follow my lead and be ready to move quickly when I do." Shaking her head Abby stepped in full view of the guards heading right for them in a drunken swagger looking over her shoulder at the others she called back loudly "See I told you I could find the vault room and you did not believe me."

Without looking to see if the others were following she headed for the row of guards in front of the doors calling out loudly "Hey, guys we got here too late to see the king display the trophy last night. You guys wouldn't mind if we took a peek would you?"

Shrugging his shoulders Fredrex stepped out into the open behind her. "Come on I think I know what she has in mind. You three stay with the Desert cats but be ready to move once we get the guards out of the way." He whispered to Buck and the two smallest members of the group. Following Fredrex's lead, the others fell in behind Abby trying to look like a drunken group of partiers.

As they neared the guards a grey-bearded man wearing what looked like golden armor stepped in front of the others. "Hold where you are strangers!" Still smiling Abby slowed her pace not stopping till she was within a few feet of the guard. Drawing his sword the man repeated his demand. "I said hold where you are women take one more step and I will run you through, this place is off limits to all but the king and his advisers." Behind him the rest of the guards drew their weapons and spread out into a half circle blocking the pathway to the vault room. "Leave now and we will let you go with a warning and your lives"

Following Abby's lead, Notie lurched forward draping an arm around Abby's shoulders grinning at the men. "We just wanted to see the diamond horse everyone was talking about we don't want to fight are you sure we can just take a peek?"

Taking a menacing step forward the man shoved the tip of his sword hard against Notie's chest. "You were warned once you drunken fool now turn around and go back into whatever bottle you crawled out of while you still can."

"Ok, ok..." Notie belched loudly throwing up his hands. "No need to get so worked up we will leave." Putting a hand on Abby's shoulder he muttered. "Come on sweet thing you want to see a trophy I will show you one back in the room."

"Pig!" Abby shouted grabbing Notie's arm and swinging him hard into the half circle of watching men catching them off guard. Frerdrex and the others were on the guards before they had a chance to recover or sound an alarm.

Jumping at the closest guard Fredrex smashed his forearm against the side of the man's face sending him slamming backwards into the wall knocking him unconscious. Looking around he saw the others guards lying scattered around the hall floor, his friends standing over them with unbloodied swords. "They all still alive?" he ask the others.

"For the time being." Vale said looking down the empty hallway "That may change if we can't stop Molder, I doubt he would be very forgiving with them for this."

Waiting as Buck and the rest of their party caught up with them Fredrex Glanced over at Notie who had one arm hanging limply at his side. "What happened to your arm, are you wounded?"

"Not by any of them," Notie said grinning. "But I think the dainty little lady here pulled my arm, out of socket when she threw me into our friends."

"Serves you right," Abby told him. "You're lucky I did not pull it clean off your body for that smart ass comment."

Fredrex shook his head sighing, "Dam Abby do you have to hurt every man you touch or are we just the lucky ones?" Not giving her time to answer he turned back to Notie "Maybe you should stand guard out here and sound the alarm if anyone shows up you're not going to be much good in a fight with that arm."

Shaking his head Notie held up his sword with his good arm. "I still have this one and there is no way I am going to miss out on whatever happens in there." He told the others

Shrugging Fredrex grunted. "Ok, if you are sure then, Come on." He told the others we need to get these men secured before they wake up, tie them up and gag them we can throw them in the storeroom down the hall."

Watching as the others drag the guards off Buck walked up to the twin doors at the end of the hallway staring at them in silence. "You do know old king that you have to push on a door to open it?" Abby Said coming up behind him.

"I know very well how to open doors girl," Buck replied with a backward glance. "But I also know that by opening these doors I could very well be leading you all to your deaths. I have caused much suffering in my life maybe it would be best if I were to do this alone."

Stepping past him Abby put a hand on each door shoving them open. "Yea, yea and I have a sore on my ass from riding in leather pants we all have our little problems, let's do this".

Ashes was almost disappointed he and Zephyr was nearing the halfway mark in the race and so far it had seemed like no more than an early morning ride. Once they had entered into the hills in the first part of the race they had lost sight of the other riders. Some had road on ahead trying to gain as much of a lead as they could others had simply disappeared into the hills. Having never run in this race before or any race for that matter he was a little confused. Was not the idea of a race for everyone to follow the same path?

Letting the rains go slack he gave China his head as the stallion carefully picked his way down a steep ridge, loses shale skidded out from under his hooves starting small avalanches in front of them. Looking back to make sure that Zephyr and Kena were not having any trouble Ashes saw a quick movement in the trees they had just passed.

Pulling the rains hard he slammed his heels into China's flanks sending the big horse jumping forward knocking Kina staggering sideways.

Zephyrs outraged yell echoed off the hillsides as he fought to keep the mare on her hooves in the loser's shale "What the hell did you do that for?"

In answer, Ashes pointed at the trees as two men raced their horses half running half sliding down the hill. "Just as I thought this was getting boring." He told the boy nodding at a shattered crossbow bolt lying in the shale.

"They say that half of the man that starts in this race never live to see the next nightfall." Zephyr said softly "And a lot of horses too."

Watching the two fleeing men and their mounts as they topped the next hillside Ashes grunted, "Well If those two are an example of what the others are like I can see why. Come on, and keep your eyes open."

After a Stop at the bottom of the hill to make sure that the horses were all right and a quick study of the terrain they headed out again at a fast trot breaking into a canter as the ground would allow.

Both China and Kenya were strong horses in the prime of their lives and Ashes was impressed by how the smaller mare was able to keep pace with the bigger stronger stallion. He was even starting to wonder what kind of foal the two would produce given the chance. If they both lived through this maybe it might be something to talk to the boy about.

Zephyrs voice pulled Ashes from his thoughts "Ashes!" Startled he looked around at the young man. Nostrils flaring Kena Stood head up and ears back both her and her rider staring hard at something moving through the trees just ahead of them. Drawing his sword He followed the sounds of branches breaking whatever was coming their way was not acting like any wild animal making no effort to be silent. That meant whatever it was did not know they were there or it did and did not care.

Straining his eyes and ears to make out the unseen foe he used one hand to signal Zephyr to stay where he was. Ashes started to ease China ahead trying to both keep track of what was moving through the trees and at the same time watch out for an ambush.

Scanning the landscape around them he spotted two fly covered unmoving lumps in the nearby grass. The rank smell of blood hit him as he recognized the bodies of the two men that had tried to ambush them. Hearing a hissing snarl he looked up instantly recognizing the huge shape that stepped out from the trees ahead and the rider on its back, Molder!

"I saw you when the race started." The dark voice said. "But I have seen you before haven't I? Back in the caverns, I told you then to leave and you did not listen to me. Do you think that I don't know why you have come? Do you truly think you can free her? If you do then you are more of a fool than the one you followed that thinks he can sneak into my chambers and steal my most cherished possession. He will soon find out how wrong he is and so will you, just before you die."

Ashes could feel China tense beneath him the stallion could sense the battle coming and was ready, the fact that this creature was a demon made no difference to him. He was confident in his strength and the strength of his rider there was no doubt in his mind that they would win.

While not quite as sure as his horse Ashes was not afraid he had fought in more battles than he could count and if he was to die in this one he could at least try to take this filth with him, or at the very least buy his friends the time they needed. Gripping China's flanks with his legs Ashes leaned forward shouting back at Zepher as the stallion charged Molder and his mount. "Get out of here boy now!"

China and Molders mount charged each other at a dead run colliding with bone-crushing force forcing Ashes to pull his leg back not to get it caught between the two huge animals. The impact knocked both horse and demon staggering sideways almost unseating their riders. Being the lighter and the more agile of the two China recovered first spinning around and planting his forefeet unleashing a kick with both powerful hind legs catching his opponent hard in the side knocking him further off balance.

Ashes grabbed a handful of mane and readied his sword as the big stallion spun around launching himself at the demon again.

Molder quickly realized that he had underestimated his foe he had expected Ashes to fight or to flee, like the others in past had. What he had not counted on was China's surprising speed and strength, the big stallion could well have a chance of defeating his own mount. A dark smile crossed Molders face, but only if his mount was what he seemed and these fools were quickly going to learn that it was not.

China closed the space between him and his enemy in two strides his mouth open ready to sink his teeth into the demons neck. Ashes braced himself readying his sword for a swing as soon as the other man came within reach. Molder and his mount stood watching not making no attempt to defend their self or move out of the way of the enraged stallions charge.

That struck Ashes as odd but with China quickly closing the gap between the two he had no time to worry about such things. Ashes put all his strength behind the swing as he and China both struck out at their foes working together as one like they had in countless battles both teeth and blade striking at the same time moving with blinding speed, to pass through their targets harmlessly as Molder and his mount melted into the ground.

Searching for his enemy Ashes twisted in the saddle, nothing moved, the dark stallion's hoof prints were the only proof that Moller had been there at all. Still wary Ashes nudged China closer to the spot where the two had vanished when the stallion suddenly jumped sideways forcing his rider to grab a handful of main to keep from losing his seat.

Regaining his balance Ashes watched in disbelief as the ground were Mulder and the demon mount had been exploded into a thousand twisting forms. China stopped staring in confusion at the ground now covered with slithering shapes moving quickly their way. Dragon serpents.

For the second time, Ashes was forced to grab a handful of main to keep his seat as Chicana suddenly reared to avoid a blurring fast strike from the nearest snake. Regaining his balance Ashes twisted around in the saddle trying to find Molder a cold laugh echoed tauntingly seemed to come from every direction at once. "You see fool do you finally understand what you face? You lost this fight before it even started."

"If you are so certain of that then face me!" Ashes shouted taking a backhanded swing at a serpent that had come within reach. "What do you have to fear? Prove how powerful you are 45fight me if you have the guts."

For a brief second, he thought that Molder was going to. Accept his challenge as the Sorcerer reappeared behind him stepping his way. "Fool. Your end could have been quick…" Stopping in mid-sentence Molder turned to stare at the City in the distance seeming to forget about the battle going on behind him. The dragon serpents gave Ashes little time to take advantage of the distraction.

The serpent's attacked with fighting speed rearing and striking China barely managed to avoid the fast strikes even as the stallion dodged one of the deadly snakes several others attacked. Leaning low in the saddle Ashes swung repeatedly at the twisting shapes giving China the chance he needed, bunching his hindquarters the stallion leaped clear of the deadly circle. As soon as his hooves touched the ground he spun rearing in mid-turn to come down full force on the closest of the snakes crushing them under hoof.

Jumping out of the saddle Ashes charged Molder on foot trusting China to deal with the Dragon serpents. The stallion was strong and fast enough to handle the snakes even if they reformed into the demon horse. Molder was the real danger, taking quick aim he put all his strength behind the throw as he threw his sword at the Sorcerer. The long blade flashed as it spun end over end to bury itself deep in the man's chest knocking him to the ground.

Hearing a startled snort Ashes looked behind him to were China stood staring at the blackened ground that had a second before been covered with twisting forms. A soft hissing sound drew his attention back to the spot where Molder had fallen his sword still stood upright its tip still buried in the now blackened ground but there was no sign of Molder or his body. Stepping carefully around the darkened ground Ashes pulled his sword free.

Jerking back his hand as he grabbed the handle even threw his gloves the coldness of the metal burned his hands. "Do you still not see?" A dark voice hissed in his ear as a cold shadow passed across his body. "Do you understand now fool why you cannot win? You are less than nothing to me not even worth my time to put an end to you. Your friend's lives are forfeit they have violated my sanctuary and I will not forgive that. But if you flee now I will spare your life. Go now! While you can."

The shadows touch left Ashes weak and angry calling to China he sheathed his sword and waited as the stallion trotted up standing for him to mount. Pulling himself up in the saddle he glared at the dark spot where Molder had been. "You are powerful but you are a fool, I don't leave my friends to die not even to save my own life, and they would not abandon me that is what makes us strong and that is why we are going to defeat you." Leaning in the saddle he slapped Chinas neck with the reins racing the stallion in a run for the city.

Chapter Ten
Rebirth of a Legend

Stepping through doorway into the vault room Abby let out a startled gasp as the ground in front of her fell away in a steep drop leveling off hundreds of feet below leaving her standing teetering on a narrow ledge overlooking a huge cavern. Strong hands grabbed her shoulders steadying her and pulling her back through the doorway.

"Careful." Clip chuckled. "I promised our parents I would keep you safe but I can't do that if you are going to jump off every cliff you see."

"Huh," Abby muttered back at her brother. "That's funny, they never ask me to promise them any such thing about you. Thanks for the save though." she added softly

Still grinning Clip let go of his sister. "You always were a lousy liar."

Stepping past the two siblings Vale cursed under his breath. "Damn this is either the biggest room ever built or we are very lost."

"We're in the right place." Buck told him. "These caverns are Molder's domain where his power is at its strongest and where he summons his dark lord to feed on the power he has stolen from Stormracer and the people of this realm. The vault room is just an illusion to fool the people if they knew what was beyond these doors he would not be sitting on the throne as their king."

Grabbing a torch from a nearby holder he light it holding it in front of him searching the jagged drop off till he spotted a narrow path crisscrossing its way down the cliff ledge. Starting down the trail he looked back at the others. "Come on we don't have much time Molder will have sensed when we entered the caverns you can bet he is on his way and I don't want to be caught with my ass hanging off a cliff when he gets here."

Following Buck, Fedrex looked back over his shoulder at Snowflake and Blueberry. "You two head back and make sure the horses are ready in case we need to leave in a hurry if things go bad don't wait for us take them and get out of here, understand?"

"I don't like being left out of this, but you are right someone needs to stay with the horses. But we won't abandon you if it looks like you are in trouble we are coming to help!" Blueberry said glaring at the bigger man.

Muttering to himself Fredrex followed Buck as he led the way down the narrow trail to the cavern floor. Once they reached the bottom of the cliff Buck pulled himself onto a large boulder and turned in a slow circle holding the torch high over his head searching the darkness. "Wouldn't it be better to look ahead of us for her old king," Notie commented. "I think we would have noticed when we passed her the way we just came."

"It is not Stormracer I am looking for. And as far as finding her goes that is the easy part, getting there in one piece could be the hard part." Buck told him "As I said this is Molder's domain and he has many followers here most of them are not human not anymore that is, we need to be on guard." Buck told him. Finishing the search he pointed at a soft glow coming from behind a nearby outcropping of rocks. "There that is where we need to get to."

"Not too far," Vale said following Bucks gaze. "About a five minute walk or it would be if not for our new friends there." He added pointing at the shadows where the light from the torch revealed several dozen rapidly approaching shapes.

"Damn!" Fredrex spat "Alright everyone stay close don't let them separate you," nodding at Buck he went on, "We will give you all the time we can, Get moving Old King, Abby you go with him watch his back take some of the Desert cats with you if he dies we lost, understand?"

Nodding Abby put a hand on Bucks' shoulder. "Like I said before old king. Let's do this."

"You keep this," Buck said tossing the torch to Notie, "It will just give us away, I can see where we are going well enough and with Mulberry and Bane with us, nothing is going to sneak up on us in the dark."

Catching the torch with one hand Notie shoved the end of it into the soft ground. "God go with you friend Buck and you as well Abby and Abby? Just in case we don't live through this, that time when we first meet and I told you I tripped when I grabbed your uhhh backside, I lied I had too much to drink that night and well..., sorry about that." Notie said with a grin before turning to join the others.

"Oh, you can bet your ass you're going to be sorry," Abby growled glaring at Notie's back.

"They left," Notie said rejoining the others.

Readying his sword Vale stared grimly at the fast approaching line of snarling shadow stalkers "It is up to them to come up with a way to free the Stormare. Our job is to buy them the time they need to do it."

"Here they come!" Fredrex shouted above the rising shriek of the shadow stalkers, "We either stop them here or we die trying there's no retreat." With a savage snarl, Cinnamon launched herself at the closest of the dark shapes, the remaining Desert cats close behind. The cavern quickly become a violent battleground both roars and yells echoing off the walls as the rest of the group joined the battle.

Calling softly to Bane and Mulberry the two hurried through the darkness barely getting a hundred yards before the sounds of battle broke out behind them unholy screams and roars mixed in with the snarls of Desert cats and the soft thunk of swords striking flesh filled the cavern. Buck and Abby shared a worried look. "That sounds like a lot of shadow stalkers," Abby said worriedly. "Maybe we should go back and help them."

Shaking his head Buck increased his pace. "No, if we do we risk everything. They are doing their part and we must do ours." Putting a hand on Bane's back he pulled himself onto the big cats back nodding at Abby to do the same with Mulberry. "They can see better in the dark than us and their far faster, just climb up and hang on don't try to guide her Bane knows which way to go and she will follow him." Following his example, Abby climbed onto Mulberry's back casting a last worried look back over her shoulder were her brother and their friends were fighting for their lives as the Desert cats raced silently through the darkness.

Needing no encouragement China covered the distance to the city with ground-eating strides demon or not, Serpents or not, the stallion had been challenged and he meant to answer that challenge. The fact that his rider was making no attempt to slow his charge told him that the man was just as eager as he was to finish this battle.

Nearing the city gates Ashes saw a large crowd of cheering people blocking the path spotting Zephyr and Kenya in the center of the crowd he realized that the young man made it safely crossed the finish line. "Good for you son," Ashes thought. "I Hope your father and brother are watching."

China only slowed his charge enough to avoid the startled townspeople who scrambled to get out of his way. Once clear of the crowd the stallion continued his headlong run to the castle and the unfinished fight with Molder's demon mount.

Ashes guided China through the city streets not having been with the others when they discussed it he had no real idea were the vault room was. He was cursing himself now for not having thought of that detail before. "Idiot that is something you might have wanted to ask about." he muttered hotly under his breath. The castle was his first guess and he was desperately hoping he was right.

Slowing China to a trot Ashes reined the stallion to a stop under a grove of oak trees a short way from the castle entrance. He had studied the castle inner walls and gates, the vault room had to be somewhere in the center but it would also have to be a large room to accommodate the crowd at the displaying of the trophy. Patting the stallions sweaty neck he guided him down the road toward the gate.

"Ashes!" Hearing his name he turned in the saddle looking for the speaker. "Over here!" Blueberry called softly from a side street, "Hurry, This way." The small man called to him as they ducked into the narrow pathway leading them to a small stable next to the guard quarters where Snowflake and the rest of the horses were waiting.

"Fredrex asked us to guard the horses in case we needed to make a run for it." He said sourly "I think he just thought we would be in the way in a fight."

"Don't sell yourself short," Ashes told him, "Fredrex ask you two to stay with the horses because he knows you two have the best chance of keeping them safe, they listen to you, I would have made the same choice. Listen to me we are out of time Molders knows what we are trying to do and is on his way to stop them. Do you know where the vault room is?"

"The vault room is in the main chambers just past the entrance way." Snowflake offered "The others went in not long ago"

"No guards?" Ashes ask

"A few," Blueberry grinned, "They're tied up in the storage closet come on I will take you to the vault room. Will you be alright alone for a few minutes?" He asked Snowflake.

"Don't worry about me I will be fine." The small women told him. "You take care of yourself," With Blueberry leading the way the two quickly made their way to the hallway leading to the vault room

"That is the way the others went in but," Blueberry stopped in mid-sentence whipping his head around both men stared at the doors at the end of the hallway.

Even threw the thick wood doors the sound of the battle could be heard. Grabbing the heavy metal handles. Ashes grunted as he pushed against the unyielding doors. "Damn it!" He snapped. "Are you sure this is the way they went?"

Standing next to him Blueberry paused in his own efforts of trying to force the doors open glaring at him "Yes this is the door they went through do you think I am so slow-witted I would forget?"

"No that's not what I was saying, stand back we can't break these doors down but I am betting he can." Ashes said nodding at the stallion. He had been tempted to leave the big horse in Snowflakes care with the others not knowing for sure what they were running into if a fight broke out in a confined space the horse's size would be a liability. He was not sure what whim of fate had made him change his mind but he was grateful for it.

Taking up the reins he turned the stallion's hindquarters to face the door after looking around to make sure Blueberry was out of the way he let out a short sharp whistle. A deafening thunder filled the hallway as China unleashed a series of powerful kicks at the door. At first, Ashes was afraid that even the stallion's strength would not be enough, the doors stubbornly refusing to open. Ears plastered flat against his head the stud put all his strength behind the last blow the force of the impact showering both men with splinters as the doors gave way.

"Good boy!" Ashes said patting the blowing horse on the neck. Picking his way thru the remains of the doors Blueberry stared in disbelief at the emptiness on the other side of the dark entrance way. The sounds of the ongoing battle reaching them from the cavern floor. Walking up beside him Ashes nodded at the footprints in the soft dirt leading down the narrow trail Swinging up into the saddle he looked down at the other man "That is the way down I am going to go help them, you head back and let Snowflake know what's happening if it looks like we failed you two take the horses and get as far away from this place as you can. Understand?"

"No, no way!" Blueberry snapped "You are going to risk both your necks riding a horse down that trail but think we are going to run and hide? I will go back and tell her what is going on and we will stay with the horses, but if we don't hear from you we are coming looking. I would sooner die fighting for my friends than run away and hide and you can bet Snowflake feels the same way!"

Sighing Ashes grinned at the young man, "Fair enough with any luck we won't have to worry about it anyway." Without another word, he nudged China in the side with a boot letting the stallion pick his own way down the dangerous pathway to the bottom.

The pathway down the cliff side was narrow, with several places where the stallion's side brushed the cliff wall, more than once Ashes questioned his decision to take the big horse. But once he started down the narrow pathway there was no turning back. Trusting the horse, he concentrated instead on the battle going on below trying to make out his friends in the twisting mass of bodies in the dark cavern.

Eager to join the battle China wasted no time working his way to down the path and surprising his rider by jumping the last several feet to land running toward the battle.

Ashes had been expecting the battle to be a savage one, what he was not expecting was to find himself in the middle of it after traveling what seemed like only a few feet. The huge boulders littering the cavern floor served to not only block a man's sight but echoed the sounds of the battle to a degree that it was almost impossible to tell what was going on and where.

Dodging around an unusually large bolder they found a blood-covered Vale and Clip surrounded by a pack of shadow stalkers. Swinging his sword in a wide arch Ashes cut the nearest one in half as China trampled two others under hoof who were to slow to get out of his way. Using the distraction both Clip and Vale helped finish off the rest.

"Not that I am unhappy to see you, But what the hell are you doing here? What about the race? And how the hell did you get a horse down here?" Vale ask staring in disbelief at China.

"Yeah, it is a long story," Ashes told him " We need to get to the others, Molder is down here somewhere I tried to stop him but he got past me we underestimated his abilities, where is Buck?" looking around he added hopefully. "Did you find the statue where is Stormracer?"

Clip looked up pausing from tying a crud bandage around a deep gash on Vales' ribs. "These damn things jumped us almost as soon as we got here so we had to split up, Buck and Abby left with two of the Desert cats to try to wake Stormracer, they headed that way." He told Ashes pointing at the soft glow in the distance. "I have not seen Molder but you can bet if he is here it is them he will be going after not us."

Ashes turned to look at the spot that Clip had indicated, the eerie light only a few minutes away on China but it might as well have been miles. The short break that they had earned passed quickly as dozens of shadow stalkers charged out of the darkness quickly surrounding them. Bringing China around to meet their charge he saw Fredrex and the rest of his friends running from the darkness to join in the battle.

There was nowhere to go and even if there had been no way he would leave his friends outnumbered and fighting for their lives like this. A cold feeling passed over him as he realized that Buck and Abby were on their own and even with the two powerful Desert cats fighting by their side they had little chance against Molder. Their fate and the fate of this world rested in the chance that they could awaken Stormracer and there was no way for any of them to know for sure if they had even found her.

Abby had seen the diamond statue years ago but as they passed the last line of boulders she let out a startled gasp of wonder as she saw it clearly for the first time. Like all the others at the presentation her vision had been clouded by Moldor's illusions seeing a grand room and not the vast caverns. And seeing a crudely carved statue, not the wonder that stood in front of them now, that threw back even the smallest spark of light like a burning sun.

Even Mulberry and Bane seemed impressed by the sight, pacing in front of the shimmering form only stopping long enough to allow their human friends to slide off their backs, "By all that is holy" Abby whispered staring in disbelief.

Buck walked past the awe stuck women. "Beautiful is it not?" He ask "But this is nothing compared to her true beauty, wait here it is time for me to correct a mistake I made fifteen hundred years ago."

Stormracer still lay on her side as he had last seen her. Her head raised, sorrow filled eyes staring...Buck walked the last few feet each step slower than the last even though they were frozen and unmoving like the rest of her he could not bring himself to look for more than a second into her eyes.

Stopping in front of the unmoving form Buck dropped down to his knees his own eyes focused on the ground in front of him, before finding the courage to raise his head and look into the eyes he had seen in his dreams every time he slept.

Memories flooded him feeling him with guilt and shame, Buck did not even try to stop the tears that they brought reaching out he wrapped his arms around the cold neck hugging it with all his strength as he pleaded through gritted teeth praying harder than he had in his life. "Please God let this be undone, I know it is wrong to ask you this, What I did ,I did with foolish pride, Take my life do what you will with me but don't let this world die. You have the power to heal you are the God of animals and man, do what you will with me but please let her run again."

Abby listened in silence she had no idea what to expect if Buck had a plan he had not shared it with her. Watching now she waited unsure what to do, of all the things she had expected Buck to try, praying was not one of them. Why not? The women ask herself right now it seemed like the only way they were going to live thru this was if God helped them. But her mother had always told her God helps those who help themselves.

Watching the pacing Desert cats she desperately tried to think of anything that she had heard on their journey here anything that might help them. Wait in the woods when they first met Ashes and Buck, what was it that Ashes said that Stormracer had told him. Running up to Buck she grabbed his shoulder startling him "Listen to me old king I need you to think clearly what was the message that Stormracer gave you?"

Buck got to his feet looking half angry. "She said that what once was can be again but first I must seek forgiveness from the one hurt most by my mistake. But do you think I have not tried that? I have asked, begged for forgiveness for the last thousand years in every way I know. The people of my kingdom are gone, Dead, I have prayed for forgiveness from them. From God, And Stormracer, Even the land itself. What more can I do, who else is there left for me to beg forgiveness from?"

Sighing Abby surprised Buck with a gentle kiss on his cheek. "You're male, so I understand your bullheadedness and denseness from what I have seen from my brother and the men I traveled with I am pretty sure it is normal. But think old king, who was truly hurt most by what happened? Stormracer? Yes, her body is trapped but her spirit still runs free how else could she have given Ashes the message? Your people? As you said they have all moved on to the next life and from what you told me yourself your brother said they did not blame you. God? I have not met him personally lately but I think he knows more than anyone what happened.

The only one I know of who has suffered and is still suffering is you old king." reaching down she took his hand in a two-handed grip squeezing hard. "For fifteen hundred years you have imprisoned yourself in a dead land blaming yourself for something that was not your fault. For what once was to be again you need to realize that Buck... You are not to blame for what happened you did not trap Stormracer, but you can free her, you are the only one who can."

For a moment neither of them spoke a look of uncertainty etched in Bucks' face as he looked from this strange woman standing in front of him to the frozen diamond form of what once was Stormracer. "When a man accepts the truth and finally understands." He whispered. Reaching into his shirt he pulled out the jewel-encrusted medallion staring almost mesmerized at it. "In a storm's fury, God will return her one day. That's it!" He yelled startling Abby. "How could I have been so foolish not to see it? You were right, don't you understand? Molder never trapped her, not entirely, her body was frozen but only her body. To someone like her, a body is a fleeting thing, the things that make her what she truly is her spirit, her power those he could never trap much less hold. All he has ever had is a lifeless statue."

"Alright." Abby said looking lost "So what does that mean? Can you free her or not?"

"Yes," Buck told her turning back to face the dark cavern. "Once all the pieces are in place and I think that the last one will be here very soon."

"The last piece?" Abby started to ask, a soft hissing sound interrupted her drawing both daggers she searched for the source of the sound as she moved closer to Buck protectively. With deep growls, Bane and Mulberry padded up to stand on either side of them lips pulled back over sharp teeth ready for battle. As almost on cue the darkness in front of Buck twisted in on itself forming a dark opening barely large enough for the huge shape and the rider that stepped out of it.

Unafraid Buck stepped closer to the newcomer. "Greetings Mulder."

Molders gave Buck a look of contempt "So the boy king has found the courage to leave his castle in the desert and challenge me, and you brought me a gift." He added leering at Abby.

"It did not go so well for you last time you tried pig!" Abby snarled. "This time I will cut off your balls and feed them to you!"

Unworried Molder studied Abby "Ahh I recognize you now, you are the female from the last race the one with the donkey, where is that animal? I owe him for the trouble he caused me."

Snarling Abby lunged at Molder only to run into Bucks outstretched arm blocking her way. "No." He told her softly. "He is trying to anger you. He draws his power from it."

Favoring Abby with a smirk Mulder looked back at Buck "Tell me little king did you truly think that you could take what is mine? Even with the help of those fools who are dying as we speak. I am far more than I was before, you had no chance against me then what chance do you think you have of beating me now?"

Not taking his eyes off the other man Buck waved the Desert cats back stepping closer to the taunting Molder and his mount. "What chance do I have of beating you? Proudly very little even with my friends help. But it is not me you need to fear it is her!"

Nearing the other man Buck raised his arm the medallion dangling from its chain in his hand catching the light reflecting from the Diamond form of Stormracer striking it and filling the cavern with a blinding light.

"NO!" Molder Yelled Slamming his heals into the side his mount trying to run Buck under its hoofed feet, the demon leaped forward with a hissing snarl the light hitting him like a solid blow unseating his rider and forcing him back till with a scream of fury he vanished back into the dark doorway he had come from.

Shielding her eyes from the blinding light Abby could barely make out Buck as he held the medallion in front of him. "I Buck, king of Brutus-hay as granted by the laws and rights of the land, call to you great mare in this time of need I Summon you, hear my call and answer, hear my call and RUN FREE ONCE MORE!"

The medallion rose on the air floating out of Bucks' hand. Stepping back to stand beside Abby and the Desert cats, Buck watched as small at first, flashes of lighting shot out from its center striking the cavern walls climbing to the ceiling like living things.

Struggling to his feet Molder watched in horror flattening himself against a nearby bolder. Spotting several shadow stalkers cowering from the lighting behind a large group of boulders he angrily pointed at Buck and Abby shouting. "Fools what are you waiting for kill them!" Reluctantly the shadow stalkers moved out from behind their shelter spreading out to surround the small group.

Watching their advance Abby stepped in front of Buck with her daggers ready as both Desert cats moved to protect and to flank their human friends. Reaching out Buck gently Pulled Abby back beside him. "It is all right, we are safe they can't hurt us now." He muttered softly. Unsure she sheathed her daggers watching the events unfold in front of them.

Within the space of a few heartbeats, the lightning bolts grew in size and power striking the walls and boulders around Buck and the others but leaving them untouched. Abby felt a moment of pity as she watched the shadow stalkers turn running trying to reach the shelter of the boulders they had been hiding behind only to vanish in a brief burst of flame as the fast-moving bolts reached them.

Growing even more powerful the bolts began moving back down the cavern walls merging into one another as they collide till only a single bolt remained moving across the cavern floor to strike the diamond form of Stormracer with blinding flash. A joy-filled whinny shook the cavern walls. "I -AM- FREE!"

Blinking away the spots in front of her eyes Abby stared in disbelief at what she saw. Nothing remained of the cavern the dark walls and ceiling, as well as the boulder covered ground, had vanished leaving her and Buck standing in a rich meadow with two confused Desert cats standing next to them.

Hearing someone yell her name she saw Clip running toward them with the rest of their party, bloody and limping but all of them still alive. Running up Clip grabbed his sister lifting her off her feet in a joyous hug. "Damn girl you did it! I thought for a second that we were not going to get through this one."

Laughing Abby shoved against her brother's chest freeing herself. "Let go of me you ass, your filthy and you smell like shadow stalkers." Looking around she spotted a terrified Molder lying on the ground fear filled eyes looking not at them but above them. Following his gaze Abby's breath caught in her throat rearing in the air above their heads was a sight She had never truly thought she would see…..Stormracer!

Buck had tried to describe her to them many times but staring at her now she realized that there were no words to describe the beauty of the mare standing in the air just over their heads. Scanning the meadow below her the mare turned sorrowful eyes on the frightened Molder. "Child, I am so sorry but there is nothing I can do to change the fate you have chosen for yourself."

Pushing himself to his feet Molder snarled at the mare. "The fate I have chosen for myself? My path was forced on me by this fools arrogant parents their whole family line." He spat pointing at Buck. "I wanted what was best for Brutus-hay what would have kept it strong but they would not listen they wanted to give away everything that made it a powerful kingdom so I did what I had to do. I chose an ally that understood and helped me achieve the power I deserve."

"The power you deserve?" Stormracer echoed "The power to destroy a land? Force people from their homes and farms?, Tear apart families? And cause unimaginable suffering? No child, no one save one, should wield such power. And he would never do so for the reasons you did."

Molder snarled. "Who are you to speak to me about abusing power? You place yourself above the people of this world reveling in their foolish admiration for you, playing with the forces of nature uncaring of the suffering that your actions bring to others save those you favor!"

Shaking her head Stormracer slowly settled to the ground. "How little you understand, So much you do not know. The power I wield is great indeed and like you and every other creature I was given the free will to use it as I wish. But I serve my God freely his word and will are my law. Unlike you I will not abuse the gift I was given, all my actions from the smallest rain shower to the mightiest hurricane are all in line of what must be. I cannot and will not work against God's will. Your destiny could have been a great one. You were given a gift that rivaled that of any king the knowledge of the mystics and the ability to wield them, but you chose to turn your back on that gift in search of a power you could not wield."

True sorrow filled her eyes as she stepped closer to Molder "As I said, child, I am truly sorry I bear you no ill. All must face trials in the paths put before them in life even myself. It is the actions you take in dealing with those trials for which you will be judged." As she was talking Stormracer moved ever closer to Molder stopping an arm's length away from the defiant man. "Forgive me child I only do what I must, you sought the power that I wield and it has been decided that you shall have it."

Standing in front of a surprised Molder Stormracer lifted a foreleg bringing it down again as a loud clap of thunder rolled across the sky. As the sky fell silent again a triumphant Molder raised a hand over his head. "I did not think you such a fool horse but you spoke the truth I can feel it. I can feel the power more than enough power to destroy even you."

Unworried Stormracer only watched as Molder raised his arm higher over his head with a triumphant shout. "Let the winds and lighting answer my call and cleanse this world of this mare and all the filth that stands in my way!"

"So much you do not understand," Stormracer said again softly." Your destiny could have been a great one child forgive me for the part I played in your fate." Stepping back she lifted her head staring at the sky above Molder "Few can wield the power you have sought, fewer still can control it."

Still sitting on China, Ashes was the first to see the rapidly approaching clouds. Lifting his head China snorted pawing the ground nervously as the nearing storm clouds drifted closer to the ground in an ever rapid spin. "Shouldn't we take shelter?" Snowflake ask. Only Stormracer seemed unsurprised by the sudden appearance of the small women and Blueberry leading the remaining horses and donkey. A small band of the city guards with them.

"You could have done so much with the power you were given nag..." Molder spat "You possess the power to challenge God himself but you wasted it. I won't be such a fool, witness in your last moments of existence what can be done by someone who is not afraid to use the Power they possess."

The sound of the spiraling winds grew deafening as the dark storm hovered above their heads pulling at the clothes of everyone standing beneath it. A look of pure hatred filled Molders face as he back away from those watching him looking up at the fast-growing tornado he shouted triumphantly, "NOW! Do as I command rid this world of this filth!"

Shaking her head Stormracer let out a soft nicker "No child, no more will suffer for your pride." Lifting her for hoof again she hesitated before bringing it down once more in a quick strike sending a rolling thunder across the valley sky. Ashes watched in awe as the hovering tornado blew apart leaving a deafening silence in its wake.

Without another word, Stormracer turned her back on Molder and made her way thru the small crowd of surprised onlookers "You think this is over nag "A furious Molder scream "You think you have won? I still possess more than enough power to deal with you."

Walking past the last of the gathered crowd Stormracer sadly glanced back one last time lifting her head to the sky "Let it end." An almost mournful whisper echoed in everyone's heads.

Before Molder could move a powerful wind struck him knocking him staggering backward regaining his balance the defiant man scream at Stormracer's retreating form. "Is that the best you can do mare, do you think I am going to run from a wind?"

Still walking Stormracer replied without looking back, "No child I do not, the wind was not meant to harm you but to keep others from harm, I take no joy in what you have brought upon your own head."

Angry beyond reason Molder started to charge her before coming to a stumbling stop. Looking down at himself, a look of horror filled his face as several almost unperceivable flashes of lightning snaked across his body. Growing in size and number they moved ever faster till the screaming man was entirely engulfed by an ever-growing ball of blinding light and heat.

Shielding their eyes the shocked onlookers backed away taking shelter behind Stormracer. 'Have no fear young ones you are in no danger." Her comforting voice filled their heads. Looking over her shoulder she raised her head blowing out twice sharply at the crackling ball of energy. That as fast as it had grown started to shrink in on itself, till with a deafening crack of thunder it exploded outwards leaving only smoldering grass were Molder had been standing moments before.

"What happened to him?" A shocked Clip whispered still looking at the spot where Molder had been standing

Stormracer's sad voice echoed softly in their heads "As I said child he was given the power that he so badly wanted, the power to shape or destroy lands. And he found out like many before him that such power cannot be easily controlled. It consumed him body and soul, Molder is no more and will never be again he is truly gone."

"Not to sound uncaring but isn't that a good thing? I mean he is gone." Notie ask.

"He was not always evil," Stormracer answered. "And all life whether good or evil should be cherished."

"So it is over, that's it, I mean once Molder was beaten and you were free wasn't that supposed to bring Brutus-hay back?" Blueberry ask looking around disappointedly.

Stormracer let out a whinnying laugh. "Brutus-hay did not come to be in the space of a day child, it took many years. And it will again, but the healing has started, the dark hold on this land is fading and the desert is already shrinking soon it will be no more. It will take time but you will see Brutus-hay in your lifetime young one" she told him

"So what happens now?" One of the guardsmen wondered, "With Molder gone who will rule Roxieca? Molder never took a queen or sired a hire that anyone knows of and he never put any kind of plan into place in case anything should happen to him. The kingdom will fall into chaos without a leader."

"Be at ease child," Stormracer said. Softly "All things were considered and planned for, your people will be cared for. Roxieca was at one time Brutus-hays closest ally and friend and many of people of this land are descendants of the people of Brutus-hay. Now that the land is free of the curse it will need a people again "Turning her head she gave Zepher a meaningful look "And a king"

"What?" A surprised Zephyr yelped "Me a king? I don't understand I am not a king I don't know anything about ruling a kingdom."

"Not yet " Stormracer agreed "But you will learn, with help and advice from friends you will become what you were born to be" Flipping her tail she looked at Buck several pairs of eyes looked from Buck to Zephyr as the rest of those watching tried to follow what was being said.

"Forgive me good mare", a surprised Buck said "But I think you are mistaken, as much as I wish otherwise I had no children Shay never conceived"

Giving Buck a sympathetic look Stormracer told him. "But she did child, sadly she did not know herself till after all had happened, she spent many sleepless nights fighting with herself knowing that more than anyone you deserved to know. But knowing as well that you would not want to bring harm to the child and at that time it would be impossible to convince you otherwise. So she chose not to tell you and to let the child think that Diego was his father for with him she bore five other children. None but the two of them knew the truth about who the boy's true father was. But standing before you now is the descendant of Buck king of Brutus-hay and the good queen Shay many times removed but of still of your blood."

"But I still don't understand." Buck said, "Why didn't Shay tell me back at the castle when we started on this journey?"

"She wanted to," Stormracer told him "But She knew that that knowledge would distract you from your goal and she knew as well that you would learn of him when it was time."

"So what does this all mean," A confused Zephyr wanted to know. "Are you really saying that I am a king?"

"A prince." Stormracer corrected him. "And an inexperienced one who will need much guidance to learn the laws and ways of a new land. Molder is gone without a leader Roxieca will fall into chaos and infighting many will die needlessly. But that can be prevented the people of your land have no knowledge of its past kings, there is no reason for them not to believe that young Zephyr is heir to the throne. Especially with loyal friends to serve as his guards and advisers.

Once Brutus-hay has recovered enough to be populated again with teaching he will be ready to assume the throne his ancestors once sat in leaving a governor to care for Roxieca both lands would prosper under such a friendship.

Looking confused Thunk ask hesitantly "Excuse me good mare, but if Brutus-hay is back, shouldn't Buck be its king?"

"No," Stormracer told him softly looking at Buck. "Some trails are far longer than others but none may walk this world forever all must one day pass into the next life."

Turning her attention to the small band of guards that had followed Blueberry and Snowflake she flicked her ears. "It is others to which the task of teaching and protecting the young prince will fall on."

Looking suddenly uncomfortable one of the men stepped forward "Your pardon good mare but we don't understand, you want us to abandon our duties and loyalties to our home for another kingdom?"

Stepping closer to the man Stormracer ask gently. 'You are Salty are you not, that is your name...ced." Surprised the man nodded Stormracer lowered head to nuzzle the man's cheek with her soft muzzle calming him. "Long ago Roxieca was Brutus-hays strongest and closest ally the people of both lands profited by that friendship. It was often said that the two kingdoms were one, there is no reason that cannot be again. The people of Roxieca have suffered much at Molders hands given a chance they will gladly welcome a new king but as I said he will need the strength, wisdom and loyalty of those who support him. You do not have to do this good man, the choice is yours but I ask you to consider the good such a union would bring to both lands."

"You are right good mare" a second guard spoke up "And I don't think many here will disagree. But there are those among the people who strongly supported Molder they are the ones who will resist the change"

I hate to say it but Powder has a point, " Salty agreed. "I mean we will do what you ask but the people will be far more willing to accept our word of what you say without argument if they could hear it from you...."

"I think you underestimate your people, " Stormracer told them. "Still perhaps there is a way. There are matters I must attend to but once done I will be allowed to run the skies once more. Tell the people of Roxieca that if they wish proof of what you say is true, that in a fortnight from this day I will greet the first rays of the morning sun over the city as a salute to the lands new king. And will ask to be allowed to walk among them as I once did and will do again in Brutus-hay."

Powder nodded his head solemnly. "We will tell the people good mare and I for one pledge my sword and life to my new Prince" One by one the rest of the guards followed suite pledging their loyalty to a stupefied Zephyr who was still trying to grasp the realization of the sudden change in his life.

"Thank you. I am not sure how much I know of being a king but I will try my best I just hope I can be a good one," he stuttered.

Surprising everyone Stormracer stepped forward lowering her head "And I am proud to pledge my services and loyalty to the new prince as well. It is a great responsibility that has been thrust upon your child but do not fear and do not doubt yourself. The blood of great kings and queen's flow thru your veins follow your heart and do not be afraid to seek the advice of your elder's child. You will make mistakes but learn from them." She glanced over at Buck meaningfully then back. "And learn from the lessons of others as well."

Pausing she lifted her head high staring over Zephyrs head ears forward as if listening to a voice none other than she could hear, with a barely perceivable node she nickered softly. "There is much still I must do children, Brutus-hay has been reborn let the life-giving rains welcome it into the world but first one last task needs to be done." Walking over to Buck she turned her side to him. "It is time good king are you ready? There are many waiting to greet you friend Buck, I will be honored to carry you to your reunion".

"Ready?" Buck said tongue-tied. "Me? Now? I mean yes of course but who will teach the boy there is a great deal he is going to need to know about Brutus-hay and what about the Desert cats and Fuzzy and Starlight Who will care for them?... Wait! ...You mean go with you? On your back? Ride you? Like my mother and all of the great kings of the past. I thought that the honor to pass into the next world with you was one that had to be earned, I am the last person who can claim to have done that!"

"The right is mine to choose who I carry into gods lands." Stormracer told him. "But tell me child who has earned that right if not the man who ruled Brutus-hay with kindness even under Molders influence? Who mourned and anguished over its loss for fifteen hundred years? And who risk everything to free me and see that land reborn? As far as the Desert cats, Fuzzy and Starlight go, their trails have not yet ended they are still needed on this world." Looking at Blueberry and Snowflake both surrounded by the imposing Desert cats who were rubbing affectionately up against their new friends she snorted softly "I think that they will be well loved and cared for in your absence child. They will miss you but they understand far more than you know and in time you will be rejoined, fear not for them."

Looking both sad and amused Buck watched the two smallest members of the party trying not to get knocked off their feet by the big cats "Is there time for me to say my farewells before we go?"

Nodding her head Stormracer watched patiently as Buck made his rounds among his friends saying his goodbyes when she noticed Thunk making his way up to her an embarrassed look on his face. "Excuse me great mare, but can I ask you a question?"

"Ask what you will child and if I can I will answer," Stormracer told him softly.

Looking more embarrassed by the minute Thunk mumbled "Well you see there is a story I heard about something that everyone keeps telling me does not exist. But I believe it does I don't know how but I just know it is real could you tell if for sure if it is?"

Having finished saying their goodbyes the rest of the group gathered around curiously making Thunk even more uncomfortable. Lowering her head Stormracer blew out a soft comforting breath. "You speak of the Firerose do you not child?"

"Uh yea. " Thunk replied trying not to feel foolish

"I will never understand why man must always seek out what they cannot have or control." Stormracer sighed. " Yes, the Firerose does exist child, but I cannot tell you where it is because I do not know. That is a matter for others you would be wise not to seek it out. But if you truly must then you need to ask the dragoness Charm of the Jubilee Mountains only she can tell you where it is hidden."

"A dragon!" Snowflake gasp "A real dragon? I thought that they had all died off a long time ago. Is she friendly?"

Turning to Buck Stormracer stood still for him to mount. "There are many of her kind that still roam this world small one, they just chose to let man think they are gone. And she is a dragoness child." She told Snowflake. "She will either tell you what you want to know or make a meal of you, dragons are unpredictable that way."

"Oh" A slightly less excited Snowflake replied "Would it help if we told her that you sent us?" she ask hopefully.

"It may child and it may not, you can but try." With Buck on her back, she nuzzled the top of a downcast Snowflakes head reassuringly. "She is an older dragoness child known for her fondness of humankind I think you will be safe enough. Now we must go, I thank all of you for what you have done and I pledge that if the need should truly arise, should any of you call on me I will answer. Safe journey children." Half rearing she leaped into the air racing across an unseen ground disappearing into a cloud-filled sky.

"Well," Fredrex said breaking the silence after the two had disappeared from sight. "What now? Do we go back to Roxieca with the new prince here or go try to find an old probably hungry dragon and ask her not to eat us?"

"You are all welcome to live in Roxieca for as long as you want." Zephyr told them "I am sure that I could find places for all of you in the court. With your help." He added looking at Salty.

Grabbing up China's rains Ashes pulled himself up on the big horse. "Not that I am ungrateful for the offer but I have other places I need to be and a long overdue reunion with someone. I am grateful to all of you if we ever meet again I am in your debt if there is anything I am able to do for you I will." Turing China's head he started off toward the distant mountains.

"Wait!" Abby called after him. "You mean you are still going to find this woman that you fell in love with and left broken hearted over twenty years ago and ask her to take you back?"

Reining China in Ashes glared back at Abby "That's not how I would word it but yes that is what I mean to do. Why?"

Grinning Abby jumped up on Brian trotting the donkey to catch up. "Because I am going with you there is not enough gold in the world to make me miss this!"

Epilogue
Joyful Reunions?

The riders made their way down the narrow mountain path leading into the valley spotted with farms, stopping at the bottom of the trail the lead rider stopped his big horse and waited as the strange group made up of riders and Desert cats gather around.

"Like I said this morning. I appreciate the thought but I think I can do this myself you don't have to come with me" Ashes grumbled sourly at the others.

"And like I said at the first." Abby grinned "I am not missing this for anything and besides you might need us to pull her off your body that is if there is enough left to save."

Glaring at the woman Ashes headed China towards the closest farm. It had been over a fortnight since Stormracer and Buck had left them and they had parted ways with the new prince of Roxieca, Zephyr, and his newly formed personal guard. In that time he had tried and failed several times to convince his new friends that he did not need their help with this task.

In all honesty, he had not tried that hard as much as he loved Summer he was still hesitant about their reunion he had played it over in his mind many times and it had never ended well for him. The way he saw it the best he could hope for was a few broken ribs and a dislocated jaw he was starting to think that maybe Molder was the lucky one.

Stopping a passing traveler they learned that they were in the right place Summer did live in the valley and was very well liked and respected. Eyeing the group warily he told them how to find her. "You can't miss her place biggest farm in the valley, takes care of it herself that is one tough lady, good with a crossbow too, but if you are planning on causing her any trouble strangers you will have the whole valley to deal with Desert cats or not." The man warned them before going on his way.

146

"'I'm starting to like this girl more and more." Abby laughed. "Going to miss you though Ashes have you picked out a grave site yet? Under that pine looks nice."

Swallowing back the first comment that came to mind Ashes trotted China in the direction the man had headed them to, Summer's farm. After passing several other travelers on the road and getting more than one worried look, Summer's farm finally came into sight. Ashes had to admit he was impressed like they had been told the farm was a big one with several large fields of corn and wheat that looked ready to be harvested. "How do you think one woman does all this by herself?' Notie ask. As they made their way down the hard packed road leading to the big farmhouse.

"She probably hires extra help at harvesting time." Fredrex grunted, "Or maybe the valley farmers work to gather and help each other with the harvest, seems like a pretty close community."

Only half listening to the conversation going on behind him Ashes suddenly reined China in as several large dogs came racing down the road at them barking warningly. Un-intimidated the desert cats moved to intercept the pack.

Slapping his leg loudly Ashes let out a sharp whistle bringing the big cats to a pacing stop as a new voice yelled out a command. "Lonesome, Whiskers, Mouse, to me, now all of you!" Snarling the dogs reluctantly turned tail to stand protectively around the women who had called them.

Ashes could only stare in disbelief at the woman standing in front of him holding a crossbow. He had tried many times to imagine she would look like after twenty years, he was not expecting this. Except for a few wrinkles and longer hair, the only thing different about her was her clothes the face glaring at him now was almost the same one he had ridden away from two decades ago.

"Hold where you are strangers!" Summer half shouted, "If it is food or shelter you need I can give you the first and tell you where to find the second. But if you are here to start trouble I promise you it will cost you, I can get at least one of you before you get me and…" Stopping midsentence she lowered the crossbow staring in disbelief as tears started in the corners of her eyes her voice shaking. "Ashes? Is it really you?"

Sliding off China Ashes headed down the pathway at a fast walk to embrace the suddenly vulnerable looking woman. Of all the ways he had thought that she would react this was not one of them. Summer had never seemed the type of person to break down like this, maybe his leaving her had hurt her more than he realized.

Reaching her he lay a gentle hand on her face wiping away the tears with a finger. "Summer I am so sorry I was so wrong..."

The butt of the crossbow slammed into his belly cutting him off midsentence and knocking the breath out of him. "Your damn right you are sorry, you ass!" Summer shouted

"Where the hell have you been? What did you think was going to happen? I was going to see you and melt in your arms? It's been twenty years Ashes TWENTY DAMN YEARS! And now you just show up like nothing happened and expect me to fall all over myself with joy? You are lucky I don't put a bolt in your ass!"

Watching from a safe distance Abby leaned back in her saddle grinning. "Oh, yea I like her."

Shaking his head Fredrex looked from Abby to Summer before giving Vale a scared look. "God help us there are two of them." He said exasperated.

"Think we should help him?" Thunk wondered.

"Best to wait and see what happens." Clip put in. "If she goes for the throat then we need to do something."

Still trying to take a decent breath Ashes overheard their conversation. Thanks a lot you asses he thought bitterly that is just what she needs right now someone to rile her up... Still, he felt some sense of satisfaction this was more the kind of welcome he had been expecting. Finally getting his breath back enough he raised a hand in defense "Sumner wait. Just wait give me time to explain, please."

Stepping back a step the glowering women calmed down slightly "Fine go ahead let's hear what you have to say, but I swear Ashes if you try to tell me you were just trying to protect me I will put a bolt in your ass."

Well, there goes that Ashes thought, taking a deep breath he told her truthfully "That is only part of the reason I left. I saw to many good men die in battles leaving behind women who loved them I did not want to hurt you that way and to be honest," He added quickly as Summer started to raise her crossbow. "I did not think I was good enough for you. I had nothing to offer you but my love and you deserved so much more. I didn't want to leave you I love you I have always loved you from the first time saw you. And that is why I left,

I knew you would be angry and hurt but I hoped that you would find another man one who could give you the life you deserve."

"Huh," Summer muttered lowering the crossbow slightly "I guess that is not the worst excuse you could have come up with but tell me something. What makes you think that the pain would be any worse hearing that my husband had been killed in battle than watching the man I loved more than life itself ride out of my life without telling me why?"

Staring into her eyes Ashes heart raced as he desperately tried to think of an answer to her question that would not hurt her even more, finally giving up. "I wanted to tell you, I swear by all that is holy I did, but I could not think of any way to do it that would not lead to something like this." Sighing he started to turn away from her, "I have faced death many times in battles but I couldn't find the courage to face you that day so I left. I was a coward I never realized that till now. I don't blame you for how you feel, I will go and let you get on with your life."

A hand came down on Ashe's shoulder as he started to turn away. "That's your answer? Run away again? If you take one more step I promise you I WILL put a bolt in your ass."

Turning back to face her Ashes saw fear and uncertainty flash in her eyes replaced by something else, Love? "What do you want me to do Summer? Tell me and I will do it. I can't change the past but I can try to give you a better future if you will let me."

Giving him a hard stare Summer raised. Her crossbow slightly. "Still a slick talker aren't you? That has always been one of the things that annoyed me about you. You are not as clever as you think Ashes."

Sighing she glanced past him at the small band of travelers silently waiting and watching the events unfold in front of them. Then at the setting sun debating with herself before lowering the crossbow. "Invited or not you are here now and I doubt you have any place to spend the night. It is going to start raining before long this time of year the storms get bad. I am not about to let ANY of you bed in my house not till we work this out but there is plenty of room in the barn for ALL of you. You can bed down there, for now, there is feed for the horses and if you are hungry you can help yourself to some eggs from the hen house and there is corn in the fields. As far as your pets go I trust that you have the means to see to that." She told them "And by that Ashes I mean I better not hear about any of the neighbors or their livestock missing." Turning she started back up the walkway to the heavy log house.

Watching her leave Ashes considered following her to try to better explain his past actions when he felt a soft hand on his arm looking around he met Abby's sympathetic eyes. "Don't." She told him, "Not yet, give her time to sort through what has happened. If she did not still care about you, you would have found out by now. Let's get some sleep and you can talk to her again in the morning."

Displaying a side of her Ashes had not seen before Abby took up his hand in hers and led the reluctant man to the barn, Lost in thought Ashes followed her hardly noticing the sudden wind bringing with it the promise of rain. Like the house, the barn was well built the tight fitting logs and heavy ceiling keeping the occupants dry and warm even in the strongest storms.

Leading the horses through the big double doors they were greeted by a loud whinny as a pair of strange horses stuck their heads over their stall doors curiously watching the newcomers. Leading China to the empty stall next to the strange horses' Ashes stopped staring in disbelief at an older brown and white stallion who was staring intently at him. Reaching out a disbelieving hand he stroked the soft nose affectingly. "Nocoma?" Ashes whispered is it really you?"

"You know that horse?" Thunk asked looking through the boards from the adjoining stall.

"Yes," Ashes told him. "I bought him for Summer twenty five years ago damn I can't believe he is still around."

"Not all horses die young," Abby grunted bitterly. "Just the ones we ride into a hail of arrows, a lot of times I think that they would have been better off if we had never learned to ride them."

"Says the women riding a one-eared scared up donkey." Clip laughed from across the barn.

"Go to hell you smart ass moron!" Abby yelled at her still laughing brother.

"All right that is enough both of you." Fredrex snapped. "It has been a long day and I am tired let's just get the horses taken care of and everyone just try to get some sleep." Mutters of agreement filled the barn as everyone but Ashes stripped their horses and found a place in the straw to bed down.

"You want me to take care of China for you or are you going to sleep standing up and make him wear his gear all night?" Abby asked with unusual gentleness in her voice.

Pulled out of his thought Ashes muttered, "No, that's ok I will get him I was just thinking."

Surprising him for the second time that night Abby leaned over giving him a soft kiss on the cheek. "Don't worry so much about it." She whispered, "She is mad right now but she still loves you it will be ok I promise." Smiling she headed for Brian's stall and her empty bedroll.

Stripping the saddle and bridle off China, Ashes started at a touch on the back of his leg. Looking around he saw several goats in the next stall one particularly curious buck with his head thrust through the gaps in the boards of the stall wall staring at him. Hearing a humming sound in the stall to his left he investigated the strange noise looking through the stall boards he saw four strange animals staring back at him.

Fine delicate wide-eyed heads sat on stout long-necked bodies and even longer legs ending in a short fluffy tail covered in long thick hair.

The strange animals almost reminded him of camels studying them he decided that strange looking as they seemed they were very pretty in their own way. "Lammas," A voice said from behind him turning he came face to face with Summer. "Their called Lammas." She repeated,

"They are cousins to camels I think. I traded a merchant out of them three years back I use them to help bring in the crops they are strong pack animals and smart as hell that's one thing they have over you." She muttered. Not sure what to say Ashes just nodded numbly, Sighing Summer took his hand, "Come on we need to talk I was going to sleep on this but there is too much that needs to be said so we might as well get it over with."

Looking over at his sleeping friends he saw Fredrex lift his head off his makeshift pillow with a knowing grin on his face as he watched Summer lead the way out of the barn Ashes in hand. Stopping at the big doors Ashes balked at the heavy rain he had not even noticed when it had started. "You want to go for a walk in a downpour?" He ask

Tugging on his hand Summer gave him a disgusted look. "Come

on don't tell me that the man who road into hundreds of battles and fought demons is scared of getting wet, come on you baby, I will protect you." Not giving him a chance to argue or delay anymore she pulled him into the warm rain.

Leading the way Summer stopped under a large apple tree and ignoring the small puddles of water there sat on a bench carved out of a long dead tree patting the space next to her in an invitation to him to join her. Deciding there was no way he could get any wetter Ashes sat beside her silently waiting for her to tell him what it was that she had brought them out here for. For several long minutes, Summer said nothing staring intently ahead at the scene in front of them a large pond surrounded by a pasture full of slumbering cows and bulls with the distant lights of other farms flickering in the farm filled valley reaching to the far-off snow-covered mountains.

"Beautiful isn't it?" She said softly "I come out here all the time even in the winter just to think and wonder about things. I used to wonder what life would have been like if you had never left and if you had got yourself killed some were trying to prove how brave you are." She said half angrily.

Falling silent she reached over taking his hand in a tight grip. "You said you did not want to hurt me Ashes but you did, you hurt me worse than anyone has ever hurt me before or ever will, I love you dammit!" she shouted suddenly. "Do you think I give a damn about how much wealth you have or what kind of life you thought you could give me?"

"I had what I wanted everything I wanted, YOU! And then you just rode away. I wondered for so long if I had done something, I blamed myself for so long. Then I started hearing the stories, you are a very well-known man, did you know that? The great mercenary who feared nothing and all the battles he had been in. I started to think maybe that was what I was to you just a conquest, and I tried to hate you for that. But I couldn't because I love you too much and I could never make myself believe that you would do such a thing. Then one day I saw you in Liberty, the town was being raided by thieves and they hired some paid warriors to put a stop to it. You were leaving with them to chase the thieves away. Remember that? You didn't see me, I was too far back in the crowd but I watched you ride out you were riding a different horse then, a small red mare"

"Buckshot." Ashes said, "A good horse she fell ill just after that nothing we tried could help her, that's when I found China."

Nodding her head Summer Mumbled, "I am sorry to hear that you lost her, I know how much you care for your horses China seems like a good horse I hope you too are together a long time. Nocoma is still around getting old though. He can't do much anymore just getting fat, Dudly my other horse does most the work now." She added absently before falling silent again.

"I thought about going to you, saying something, but I couldn't bring myself to do it, Foolish huh? I mean here I am telling you what an ass you were for leaving me and then when I had the chance to be with you again I did not do it, and you want to know something? I don't know why I still cannot tell you why, I just stood there maybe I was afraid of what you might say, to hear the words that I could not bear that you did not love me."

"Summer that's not true!" Ashes told her passionately.

'I know that." Summer whispered. And I do somewhat understand why you left…" Pausing she stared thoughtfully at the sleeping cows. "I had a visitor not long ago, she knew you."

Suddenly wary Ashes tried to figure out who her visitor might have been. "She?"

Laughing Summer squeezed his hand harder. "Relax you, oaf, you think I don't know you have been with other women in the last twenty years? And anyway I don't think she would be interested in you, it was a mare a very pretty mare. You know you never ask me how I knew about the demons."

Surprised Ashes realized she was right the thought had never occurred to him. There was no way for her to know what had happened, not without being told and there was only one who could have done that. "Stormracer?" He ask already knowing the answer.

Nodding Sumner gave him a hard stare "She told me what you did, everything, she said you risk your life again and again, to help King Buck free her. She told me other things that happened as well she really likes you Ashes she ask me to give you another chance. To give both of us another chance I would have done it any way I think. But seeing her and hearing what she had to say.....made me realize that we both share the blame for what happened."

Confused Ashes struggled to make sense of what she saying, "Sumner what happened was not your fault I left you ....."

"Don't!" She snapped putting a hand over his mouth. "If you talk you are going to say something to make me mad so just shut up and listen"

Taking her hand away from his mouth she stared thoughtfully into his eyes before going on. "I don't want to lose you again Ashes I don't know if I could stand that kind of hurt again so I am asking you, do you want a life with me? I Mean here on this farm maybe a family if we are not too old, not a life out there somewhere." She said pointing at the far-off mountains. "Looking for the next battle or war which by the way, could be your last. Are you willing to give up the life of a mercenary for that of a husband and farmer? If not say so now and I will understand I will still love you but I won't try to hold you in one place if that is not what you want. I can be your friend and lover or I can be your wife, either way, I will love you but I need to know now Ashes."

Leaning forward Ashes pulled her closer to him giving her a long gentle kiss. Before letting her go "Sorry about that he grinned but it seemed like the only way to get you to stop talking. And before you start looking around for something to stab me with, the answer is I came here looking for you because I realized what a fool I have been and now I am with you I have no intention of ever leaving you again."

Snuggling tighter against his side Sumner mumbled tiredly. "You're not forgiven yet, but that's a start I suppose." Standing suddenly she reached out grabbing Ashes hand pulling on it. "Come on, I like the rain but we must look like two fools sitting out in it this long let's get back to the cabin and get dry. There is still a lot we need to discuss but we can do that after we get a good night sleep." Tugging on his hand she noticed that Ashes was no longer listening to her but staring at something behind her.

Half annoyed at him she turned searching the pasture trying to find what it was that had him so distracted when a soft voice echoed in her head.

"Greetings young ones, things are well?" Turning her gaze upward she saw Stormracer standing in the air just above the heard.

"Greetings good mare" Ashes replied dipping his head respectfully. "Yes, things are well thanks to you."

Nickering knowingly Stormracer flicked her tail. "My part in all things is small and there is much healing to be done both in Brutushay and here, but the healing has begun."

"How is Buck?" Ashes ask putting an arm around Summers' shoulders...

"He is content," Stormracer replied. He is with those he loves again and has begun his new life in Gods lands. He sends his thanks and love as well."

"Love?" Summer grinned, laughing at Ashes. "Just what went on in your little quest?"

"Quiet!" Ashes growled, "That is not funny."

Shaking her head Stormracer let out a nickering laugh of her own. "She understands the meaning of what was said child have no fear." Looking up at the cloud covered sky she sighed. "Sadly friend Ashes I must leave for now but always remember should the need arise you but have to call and I will answer, farewell and much blessings young ones." Rearing in the air she galloped over their heads vanishing into the rain filled night leaving the two of them staring at an empty sky.

"Come on," Summer said pulling on his hand. "I am starting to grow gills let's get inside I could use a warm meal and bed right now."

"Bed?" Ashes Ask hopefully. "The two of us?"

Stopping Summer turned giving him a stern look. "Don't push your luck, Stormracer got you back in my life and your apology got you back in my home but it is going to take one hell of a lot of begging on your part for you to get back into my bed. You're sleeping on the cot and if you're lucky I will throw you a spare blanket, take it or leave it. There is still the barn." Turning she headed back up the path to the cabin with a grinning Ashes following behind

"Oh yea," He thought. "Molder was the lucky one."